ONE HUNDRED PLACES

Pedro Vasquez

New York

PEDRO VASQUEZ

ISBN-13: 978-0-9979133-0-9

Other works by this author:

Novels:
Navy One
Vetting Matilda (upcoming)

Non-fiction:
Letters to America

ONE HUNDRED PLACES

Based on the screenplay
"One Hundred Places"
by
Pedro Vásquez &
Samuel J. Johnson

PEDRO VASQUEZ

To the misunderstood among us.

ONE HUNDRED PLACES

CONTENTS

One Hundred Places

PART I

Blue skies.

"I know that my mother will someday return to be part of another star, in about six billion years, when our own sun explodes and scatters our matter to other areas of the solar system."

As John's voice faded away, white streaks materialized against the blue sky. The outline of an airplane was discernible just ahead of where the contrails began.

John lay on the grass, hands folded under his head. He was turning thirty that day.

"It's time, John," said a male voice, and John, who years ago had been diagnosed with Asperger's Syndrome, did not move.

"John. Please, come in."

John kept chewing on the same piece of gum he had being chewing on for upwards of one hour. His mind seemed to wander as he stared at the sky.

A cake was set on the kitchen table across from a much-younger-looking John. Rays from a mid-afternoon sun filtered in through half-drawn curtains. Pulling the cake closer to him, John blew out the two number-shaped candles that betrayed his age. It was twelve days before the autumnal equinox, and he was turning eighteen.

Lily, a frail-looking, wheelchair-bound brunette, handed John a gift-wrapped packet, which he began to open immediately as the forty-six-year-old Lily snapped pictures with John's disposable camera.

It was a book. *One Hundred Places to See in America Before You Die.*

John's eyes shone with the innocence of someone much younger. He looked excited as he stirred in his chair. "You got it for me," he said, and he rose. "Thanks, Ma."

Lily smiled as John stooped down and wrapped his arms around her. "Anything for my big boy," she said.

Sitting back down, John began to page through the book.

"Promise me you'll go to every one of those places one day," Lily said.

John gave her a couple of quick nods. His eyes filled with doubt.

Lily said, "I reckon you'll visit every state in the union one day." John gulped.

In the town's only fast-food joint, a few patrons ate hamburgers while others nursed large sodas. It was almost 9:00 p.m., and John was pulling full-to-the-brim trash bags out of two large containers. After replacing a new trash bag in each container, he carried the bags out through a back door.

The last of the customers left, and John locked the front door and grabbed a broom that was leaning against the soda machine. He swept the floor as his supervisor fiddled with the single cash register in the place.

The supervisor pointed at the clock several moments later. "You need to hurry," he said.

John, who was still rearranging the chairs under the tables, gave a quick nod at the man before glancing toward the front door.

ONE HUNDRED PLACES

John exited the restaurant a while later, a backpack slung over his shoulder. He walked around the back of a car that had been idling near the entrance.

Lily leaned sideways as she drove out of the parking lot. John, who was riding shotgun, met her halfway. Their heads touched briefly.

"How's my boy?" she said after giving him a peck on the cheek. John sighed, and then, a smile.

"What are you doing up, Sam?" he said looking toward the rear of the car.

"What kind of question is that?" said forty-seven-year-old Samantha, an old friend of the family. Sitting toward the middle on the backseat, she was leaning forward as she spoke.

"I'm just kidding," John said, and Samantha gave him a playful smack on the side of the head. "Ma," he said, "she hit me." As Samantha ruffled John's hair, Lily, smiling to herself and without looking at him, said,

"I was just telling Sam that we're gonna have to get you a driver's license one of these days."

"It isn't right, John," said Samantha, "that we have to go to bed late every night just because you won't learn to drive."

"I wouldn't have to pick you up if you had a license, hon," Lily said. This part of the conversation seemed to make John anxious.

After she'd let him fidget in his seat a few moments, Lily reached over and stroke John's shoulder. He calmed down almost immediately. "We're just kidding, hon," she said to him as Samantha giggled behind them. "As long as I am still in this world, you don't have to worry about a thing," Lily added, and a nervous laugh issued from John.

In the dead of winter, several months later, two s-shaped rows of hay that had been placed ten feet apart from each other extended for a hundred feet over a foothill at the back of Lily's house. An early-'70s Oldsmobile station wagon with

3

exterior woodgrain panels sat idling. John, his face drenched in sweat despite it being less than forty-five degrees outside, was behind the wheel. In the daylight, the interior door-panels and the dashboard of Lily's old car resembled a bulletin board. It was filled with Post-it notes. The notes read, among other things: *Gas tank on the right, Premium only, Adjust the mirrors, Don't forget to pick up John, No hitchhikers!*

Lily maneuvered her motorized wheelchair close to the car. After plopping her overweight frame on the passenger seat, she turned toward John, who had kept staring ahead motionless. "Come on, hon," she said. "You can do this."

The car lurched forward when John stepped on the gas. Even at low speeds, he could not keep it centered on the hay 'highway.' He crashed whenever he reached a curve.

Spring came.

Just as before, John was behind the wheel in Lily's car. She sat at his side patiently giving him instructions.

"Let's try again," she said. "Steady now."

A lurch forward.

Moments of steady driving.

Another crash.

After many unsuccessful attempts, John would manage to navigate the entire stretch without crashing.

"Let's do it again, only ten miles faster this time," Lily said. "Hon, come on. You can do it."

After each successive increase in speed, it would take John about four to five tries before he could maneuver the Oldsmobile through the entire course without crashing. But he finally got it.

"You see?" Lily said, and John relaxed. He laughed even. Lily laughed with him.

John sat at the kitchen table, big grin on his face.

"Wasn't that something?" Lily said. She was beaming as she pulled him down and planted a big kiss on his forehead.

4

ONE HUNDRED PLACES

She drove her wheelchair to the counter, where she poured two spoonfuls of jelly from a jar onto a plate. Getting a clean spoon, she poured the same amount of peanut butter from another jar onto the plate. "You did well today," she said as she set two plates in front of John on the table, the spoons on either side. After ruffling his hair, she left the room.

Four slices of bread were on one of the plates. The second plate had the peanut butter on one side, near the rim; one hundred and eighty degrees opposite the peanut butter, was the jelly. The peanut butter and the jelly did not touch. John turned the plate so that the peanut butter was on the right side of the plate. Grabbing a spoon, he ate some of the peanut butter before taking a bite from one of the slices of bread. He then rotated the plate so that the jelly was on the right side. He took the second spoon and repeated the process with the jelly. The ritual continued like this, with him alternating between the peanut butter and the jelly, until both plates were empty.

Late afternoon a few days later.

A morose John was sitting outside on the steps that led straight into the living room of his mother's house. Nearby and almost straight across from him, was Lily. She was reclining in an old armchair, under a tree, and saying to him in between fits of coughing, "Not for my sake, hon." She began to get herself out of the armchair as she spoke. "I'd gladly go on picking you up." She sat her bottom on the wheelchair, which had been parked by her side all along. "That's not a problem for me." John squirmed as she maneuvered the wheelchair closer to him. She said, "I ordered that book for you because I thought that maybe…"

"I'll do it, Ma," John said suddenly. "I'll do it."

Still coughing, she reached and stroked her son's knee. The moment he glanced away, she smiled to herself.

5

Mid-morning the following day, droplets of sweat were running down John's forehead as he drove the one car in the town's driving-school pool.

In the passenger seat was Richard. In his fifties, the Department of Motor Vehicle employee was conducting John's first driving test. He scribbled on a clipboard with his left hand and held a cup of coffee with the other. Richard had worked for the DMV for far too long, and conducting these tests was the highlight of his day.

John approached an intersection and ignored the stop sign.

Another car screeched to a halt. It ended up mere inches from Richard, who could not hide the fact that he was scared.

About a week later, John was again behind the wheel of the driving-school car as he took his test a second time. On this occasion, when he drove up to the same intersection as before, he slammed on the brakes.

Hot coffee spilled all over Richard's clipboard as the cup flew out of his hand. He squirmed arrhythmically as the liquid dripped onto his crotch. John looked mortified.

"Don't worry about it," Richard said through clenched teeth. "You'll do better next time."

Richard waved at Lily as he dropped John off in front of the house moments later.

In his room that night, John looked like he was already well past his bed time as he went to turn off the lights. The book Lily had given him as a birthday gift lay next to the lamp on the night table. John picked it up and examined the cover for a few moments. Sitting up in bed, he set his back against the headboard. It was close to 3:00 a.m. by the time he set the book back on the night table and turned off the lights.

ONE HUNDRED PLACES

Early in the morning the following week, Lily was once again dropping John off in front of the driving-school building. "Better luck today, hon," she said before driving away. John waved at her for quite a while, and only after the car had disappeared around a corner did he drag himself to the building entrance.

John, his face sweaty, was sitting behind the wheel of the driving-school car for the third time.

"We don't have all day, John," said Richard from the passenger seat. John didn't move.

About thirty minutes later, Richard was sipping at his coffee as John drove on the highway. Apparently, he was getting the hang of it.

It was almost dusk on a different day.

John knocked down a safety cone behind him as he tried to parallel-park. The car lurched forward and knocked down another cone.

Richard, who had been standing outside next to the car, looked more than a bit disappointed. He raised a finger: Wait. He went to get his coffee cup from the sidewalk on the opposite side of the street.

As he was driving on a two-lane highway, John swerved away from the double yellow lines whenever another car passed him going in the opposite direction. At one point, he overcompensated as he went to overtake a school bus.

Richard held on to his coffee cup with both hands and kept it level as the Oldsmobile's left tires skidded over the gravel on the side of the road. "Let's just go back, John," he said.

"Ma said I can do it. It's just…"

"I know, John," Richard said. "But let's give it a rest for today, okay? We can always try again another day."

"But I need a license."

Although Richard shrugged, he did seem a tad sad for John.

John was fidgety when he and Lily were eating dinner that evening. Looking truly embarrassed, he said,

"Sorry, Ma."

"Don't you worry about a thing, hon," Lily told him. She started stroking his shoulder, and, soon, he looked more relaxed. "You know how to drive," she said. "Who said you have to have a license anyway?"

"The police will arrest me," said John. He sounded defeated.

"No, they won't," Lily said. "You now have a driving permit." John didn't seem too convinced. "Besides," Lily said, "everybody here knows you're my boy." When it looked like John still wasn't reassured, she said to him, "Just be extra careful when you leave town. Don't get stopped by the police."

John said, "I don't need to leave town, Ma."

"That's true," said Lily. "But you must, sweetie. We shouldn't live our lives in hiding."

Staring at the empty plate in front of him, John did not appear to be listening anymore.

"John," a male voice was saying.

Thirty-year-old John lay on the grass, hands folded under his head. He was still looking at the blue sky, where the outline of an airplane was discernible just ahead of white contrails.

"John," the paternal-sounding voice said once again. "Please, come in." John turned his head toward it.

A priest stood on the threshold of one of the side-doors of his chapel.

ONE HUNDRED PLACES

In the chapel, moments later, the priest was scanning the small congregation as he was getting ready to officiate over a funeral service.

Samantha, Lily's good friend, was sitting in the front row, next to John, whose eyes had fixed upon the casket in front of him.

The priest had already opened his mouth and was about to begin his sermon when he stopped suddenly.

John was crossing toward the casket. He retrieved a disposable camera from his pocket, snapped a couple of pictures of Lily's face.

The priest seemed sad as he regarded John, who was returning to his seat.

Two rows behind John and Samantha, three older ladies—Helen, Ariadne, and Iris—were whispering to each other. Unbeknownst to them, their whispers reached the front row, where it was obvious that John could hear them. Squinting his eyes, he appeared to consider their words.

At the cemetery, about one hour later, John and some of the funeral service attendees gathered on one side of Lily's grave. The priest stood across from them on the other side.

"We've gathered here today to remember a flower that was snatched from us too soon," said the latter. "Lily was taken by our Lord and returned to Him..." His voice trailed off.

Several moments later, Samantha said, "See you at the house, John." She was walking behind Helen, Ariadne, and Iris as the four of them made their way toward a path that led to the gate of the cemetery.

Early that evening, the funeral attendees had gathered for a potluck at Lily's house. John was sitting on an old sofa in a corner of the living room. Samantha sat across from him on an identical sofa.

9

"You know, John?" she said. "Lily's in a better place now. Don't you worry about her. I think—"

"I'm not worried," John said and, although he had cut her off, Samantha smiled at him. He said, "Right here, on this sofa. This is where I watched The Cosmos, with Carl Sagan."

Intent on him, Samantha listened to John as if he were the most important person in the world.

"He said that we're made of matter from exploding supernovas and particles from the big bang." He set his eyes on several pictures that hung on the wall, behind Samantha. One of them was of Lily. She was cradling a baby, and a man was standing at her side. In another picture, a five-year-old John played in a backyard. A third photograph showed a teenage John holding up a high-school certificate.

John did not even make eye contact with Samantha as he continued talking. He kept looking at the pictures, instead. "I know there's no significance to the fact that I buried Ma on my birthday. I also know that someday she'll return to be part of another star; in about six billion years, when our own sun explodes and scatters our matter to other areas of the solar system, maybe as far as tens of thousands of light years, before it's recycled into a new star."

When the muffled conversation of Helen, Ariadne, and Iris drifted in from the living room, John began to twiddle his thumbs, eyes downcast.

Samantha's countenance turned sad as she regarded him. John raised his gaze again after a moment, kept looking at the wall behind her.

Correspondence and trade-school certificates hung side-by-side with the pictures: 'auto-mechanics,' 'electro-mechanics,' among others. John's name was printed on all of them.

Several weeks later, John looked nervous as he stood next to Samantha in front of the house. Movers from a state charity were carrying Lily's clothes and other household items out of the house and putting them in a truck.

10

ONE HUNDRED PLACES

"She wanted what's best for you, John," Samantha was saying. John's brow furrowed somewhat. "I'm sure that's why she did it," Samantha said. "Besides, you know your uncle. He's always wanted this property." When John nodded, she added, "You should look at the positive side. It'll do you good to get out of this God-forsaken place." John became fidgety when he heard this. "There's nothing for you here, John."

That night, John was in the living room packaging the remaining items in the house. He looked exhausted as he stacked the last of the boxes against a wall; it didn't take long for him to fall asleep when he laid himself on the sofa.

John got up early the next morning. Dressed in an old pair of overalls, he ate his usual peanut butter, jelly, and bread, not-combined-as-a-sandwich breakfast.

Afterwards, he hauled several trash bags out of the house and trudged toward the road, where a dumpster was sitting just outside the fence. He deposited the bags in it and rushed back into the house.

Moments later, he brought out more bags. The lid on the dumpster did not close all the way after he had placed the extra bags inside.

John's head bobbed up at the entrance to the attic. He squeezed an arm in and reached for several items which were scattered about in there. Although the hand seemed familiar with the place, it was evident that his big frame had not fit in here for a while. Only a tenuous amount of lighting penetrated through the dirty skylight above him. He was, nevertheless, able to spot an old book that was covered in dust. Grabbing it, he wiped it off on his overalls. He looked both amused and sad at the same time when he saw the cover:

11

PEDRO VASQUEZ

One Hundred Places to See in America Before You Die. It was the book Lily had given him more than ten years before for his 18th birthday.

John stood at the foot of the attic ladder in the kitchen. He stayed there several moments, eyes fixed on the book, before letting go of the ladder. As the ladder went up into the ceiling, he looked about him.

The kitchen was bare. There was nothing in the living room either—except for a pair of heavy trash bags by the front door.

John had the book clutched under his arm as he and Samantha carried the trash bags down the front steps of the house a few minutes later.

"I thought you were never gonna come out of that house," said John's uncle. "Better hurry."

Uncle Bonnie was a heavy-set man of about fifty-five. He was plumped down in the old armchair that lived under a tree in front of Lily's house.

"I was afraid I was gonna have to get you out of there myself," he said as John and Samantha set the last of the trash bags by the dumpster outside the fence. She chuckled when John said,

"Those steps would break."

Uncle Bonnie made a face momentarily. He waved in front of him some papers he had been holding in his chunky hands.

"Watch it," Samantha whispered to John. "He's not a good man." Crossing toward where his uncle was standing, John said,

"They're too old, those steps, you know?"

"Come sign these before I change my mind," said Uncle Bonnie. Samantha scowled at the man awhile, after which she headed down the road, to her house.

ONE HUNDRED PLACES

The Oldsmobile was parked in front of Lily's house. So, when John took the papers that his uncle was offering him, he crossed over to the car and laid them on the hood. Uncle Bonnie rubbed his hands together as he watched his nephew read every page.

"Do you think this is enough for this big house, Uncle Bonnie? Where is the other ten grand?"

Uncle Bonnie said, "Eight is all I can do." As John scratched his head, the older man said, "You forget I paid for the burial? I'm letting you keep the car too, John. You're the one ripping me off."

Something in Uncle Bonnie's face betrayed quite the opposite. He waved a pen in front of John. No sooner had John finished signing the papers, than Uncle Bonnie snatched them from him, saying,

"Why don't you come to California sometime? Live with your family a while?"

John said, "Ma was my family."

Uncle Bonnie appeared taken aback momentarily, but he recovered nicely. "What you gonna do with all that cash?" He was handing John a battered brown briefcase.

"Spend it," John said. "I'll be all over the place." He waved his book in front of him in the same manner Uncle Bonnie had the pen before. "I'm going on a road trip."

"You be careful out there, son," Uncle Bonnie said. The smile he gave his nephew seemed light years from sincere.

It was mid-afternoon, and Uncle Bonnie had left. John was sitting in the driver seat of the Oldsmobile, his feet planted outside on the ground. Resting his elbows on the car door, he took several pictures of Lily's old house; the house where he had taken his first baby steps, where he became a man. He let out a sigh as he brought his feet into the car and straightened himself behind the wheel.

Two minutes later, he honked as he drove slowly past Samantha's house. She exited onto the porch. After resting her clasped hands on her lips momentarily—she seemed worried for him—she raised them in front of her: Good bye. Good luck.

John glanced about the cemetery. It was just before sunset, and there was no one else around. Lowering himself to the ground, he lay there, alongside Lily's grave.

John was listening to National Public Radio (NPR)—his favorite station—as he was driving his mother's old Oldsmobile out of town, the setting sun almost straight in front of him. The 'Talk of the Nation' segment on at the time revolved around the disagreement between Latin-America Defense Ministers and the United States regarding 'Plan Colombia.' A piece of paper was taped to the dashboard, near the radio, the letters 'NPR' underlined at the top. A list of call letters and frequencies followed.

The Oldsmobile passed the city limits. 'Thank you for visiting Ulysses, Kansas, (pop. 5,525),' read a sign on the road. There was a melancholic expression on John's face when his foot tentatively stepped on the gas. Little by little, the car accelerated.

John was driving on US-50W, through Colorado. A jar of peanut butter and another of jelly lay next to two plastic spoons on the passenger seat. Everything had been arranged neatly on top of a tray made from a torn brown paper bag.

John reached into the glove compartment for some gum. His face was a mix of wonder and apprehension when he straightened himself behind the wheel and looked at the road ahead of him.

Late that night, the Oldsmobile was parked on the side of the road—a bit too close to it. As John slept, the car swayed each time an eighteen-wheeler or another large vehicle sped past it.

ONE HUNDRED PLACES

Time went by, and judging by John's aspect as he woke up, dawn had arrived too soon. He followed US-160W to New Mexico, then took NM-59 and headed toward Utah.

It was late afternoon by the time John stopped the car on the side of the road once again. He was now within walking distance of the Four Corners Monument, in Arizona; however, he stayed in the car. Looking tired, he stared through the windshield at the hundreds of tourists that were walking about at the site of the monument. Some of them were taking pictures. He seemed confused as he watched some of the tourists get on all fours. He didn't know that people did this so they could then say that they had been 'in all four places at the same time.' He took two pictures with his disposable camera, then reached on top of the dashboard for his book. After finding the page where Four Corners was listed, he glanced at the actual monument once again before check-marking the page. He also stuck a Post-it note on it. He pushed his back against the seat's backrest, closed his eyes. But he seemed uncomfortable. He ran his hands along the sides of the seat as if he were looking for something. The backrest reclined suddenly, and he fell backward, which seemed to amuse him. He fell asleep within five minutes.

Knock, knock.

John stirred in his sleep about three hours later at the muffled sound of, "Anybody home?" The male voice came from outside the car just as a beam of light shone in through the driver-side window. He sat up as the light hit his face, and when he went to reach for the door handle, the voice said, "Stop. Just lower the window." John straightened up on the seat and ran his hand along one side of it. The backrest sprang to the upright position and slapped his back. He seemed anxious when he rolled down the window and saw the lanky police officer.

"I fell asleep, officer," he said, his voice cracking somewhat.

"You can't stay here," said the police officer. "License and registration please."

Several minutes later, John looked confused when the police officer offered him a clipboard and pen. As the seconds ticked by, he only became more nervous. The police officer said,

"Please, sign." John appeared not to register the police officer's tone of voice—it sounded rather flat—as he told him, "You need to find a hotel." John stared at the police officer. It was all he could do: he lacked the capacity to decipher facial expressions. He signed. Having retrieved his clipboard and pen, the police officer handed John a ticket and said, "I'm not giving you a parking fine."

"No?" said John sounding surprised.

"You're being fined only for driving without a proper license." He regarded John an instant before adding, "Get that taken care of." John swallowed air. "Move on now." John nodded repeatedly and fumbled his keys when he went to feel for the keyhole on the steering column of the Oldsmobile. He watched through the windshield as the police officer marched toward a van that was parked several yards away in front of him. When the car started, he wasted no time in getting back on the road.

He stopped for gas, bread, and soda along the way, and as he continued on US-160W, he ate a PB&J 'sandwich.' (It wasn't really a sandwich, but that's what he liked to call it.) He gulped some soda in between bites. He merged onto US-89S and followed it to US-180W. Several hours later, he stopped at a roadside motel.

The following day, John got on AZ-64W. As he drove through the Grand Canyon, he stopped several times to watch families on mule rides. Some of them raised a hand in greeting, and he waved back self-consciously.

He drove through a traffic circle and continued onto US-180S. An hour later, he began to follow I-40W, which would take him to California. In Sacramento, he took I-158W and followed it to San Francisco. It was night by the time he drove over the Golden Gate Bridge, a fact he apparently did not register.

Having stopped at a roadside motel two hours later, he accompanied yet another PB&J 'sandwich' with a soda before taking a shower and getting into bed. It was midmorning when he got up the following day.

The Oldsmobile was parked near the Golden Gate Bridge. John was watching from the shore as tourists rode tour boats under the bridge. He spent awhile examining his disposable camera and, in the end, took only a single picture of the scene. Getting back in the car, he drove for hours on US-101N before stopping at a rest area. He strolled for a while within sight of the Oldsmobile, then came to fish the camera out of his backpack. About to take a picture of the place, he changed his mind and got back in the car.

There was no one else around when John parked near one of the trail-heads at Redwood National Forest later that day. He had his backpack with him as he exited the car, which he locked before crossing to one of two porta-potties that were fastened to the chain-link fence at each side of the entrance to the park.

John perked up when, moments later, from his perch on the toilet seat, he heard what sounded like a person inflicting violence on another. They seemed to be just outside his door. Something hit against the exterior of the makeshift restroom, and he set his palms against the sidewalls. He waited several moments as the sound of slaps and yelling kept drifting into the porta-potty.

The moment John opened the door and saw what was happening, he tensed up, panic washing over him.

A young man was yanking a young woman away and dragging her toward a Honda Civic fourth-generation that was parked between where John now stood and the Oldsmobile. Opening the passenger door, the young man tried to push the young woman inside, but the latter set her elbow against the car frame. She held on to the door with her other hand and refused to get in.

John's eyes darted from one side to the other in their sockets as he scanned the space in front of him. But when he went for it, he could not avoid getting within striking distance of the couple.

The young woman broke free momentarily, but the young man pulled her back. He flung her against the car, half-tearing one of the long-sleeves of her blouse at the shoulder seam in the process. She reached up and covered herself as best she could when she landed in a heap on the ground. The young man grabbed her by the hair and pulled her head toward the ground when she went to sit up. He said to her,

"See what you make me do? You know I just want what's best for you—for us." The young woman managed to turn her head. She gave him a fierce stare as she wiped dust off her cheek. He gulped. "We're in this together." Looking desperate, she grabbed his hands and tried to pry them off her, but he was stronger than she. Unable to break free in this manner, she resorted to biting his legs. It worked. "You, b—!" screamed the young man making his hand into a fist as she got back to her feet. She was backing away when she ran into John, whom neither of them had noticed up to that point. She turned her head and looked up. "Come here," said the young man sounding more like a parent talking to a child than a man addressing his significant other. But his

18

demeanor changed the moment he saw John. Amazingly, the coward raised his hands in front of him, palms away from chest, in an I-don't-want-any-trouble gesture. By now, the young woman had stepped behind John, who looked as agitated as she and the young man were—if not more. John said,

"What's the problem? Why don't you leave her alone?" John's large physique provided the right incentive for the young man to back down.

"Is that what you want, baby?" he said, and the young woman hesitated after having stuck her head out from behind John.

"Yes," she said. "I think?"

The young man said, "Gonna start thinking now, baby? You're not well. Can't think straight."

"Can't think straight," she said. And then something strange happened. She looked up for an instant, and a whisper issued from her lips. "I'm gonna get well. I gotta get well."

"Suit yourself," said the young man turning to go, adding without looking back, "Don't come begging me to take you back."

The young woman gulped, and her voice, barely audible as she said, "I shouldn't," grew louder when she told him, "I won't."

A backpack flew out of the Honda Civic moments later as the young man sped away. When John moved to retrieve it, the young woman went to sit down on a bench. She was looking away when he placed the backpack at her side before crossing toward the Oldsmobile.

Although only in her mid-twenties, Nessa looked much older. There was an aura of negative predisposition about her. Her lips were broken, and her face showed bruises old and new. Her hand trembled as she sucked in a long drag from a cigarette she had just lit and which she was holding with the counter-culturish *je ne sais quoi* of a once-famous exsomething who was now a junkie. And she seemed to be suffering from a severe bout of the jitters, too. Despite all this, however, Nessa seemed blasé about being there alone with a stranger. John was about to get in his car when she called out, "Hey." He didn't look back. "Hey!"

John turned around. "Yes?" He looked disheveled from days of almost-solid driving.

"What are you doing out here?" she said.

"Me?" he said. "Nothing. Just passing through *the famous Redwood Forest!*" He had sounded like an announcer in one of those TV commercials of not-so-great quality.

Furrowing her brow in confusion, Nessa said, "You holding?"

"The keys to my mother's nineteen-seventy-six Oldsmobile," said John. "It has an eleven-point-six-liter, V-six engine. She puts only premium in the tank."

"Who?" Nessa said. "No, jackass. You have any smack?" He said,

"Why do you want me to smack you? I don't like fighting. Besides, Ma said that a man should never hit a woman, regardless of how shrill she may sound."

"Fucking heroine, dude. Jesus! You a damn cop?"

John said, "Oh, no. Ha, ha. Me a cop? Do you mean Diacetyl Morphine, synthetic derivative of morphine?"

Nessa was shaking her head from side to side.

"Diacetyl means that there are two acetyl groups in it. They help the drug move faster from the blood stream to the brain, where it attaches itself to the opioid receptors in there." Her jaw dropped. "The brain has many receptors—in the limbic system, for example." She was about to speak, but John did not give her the chance. "Did you know that it's through the limbic system that we humans experience happiness and fearlessness?" Nessa ran a hand through her hair as he continued. "It also allows us to endure pain. Morphine makes people who use it feel very relaxed."

She said, "I will take that as a no."

ONE HUNDRED PLACES

"No what?" John said.

"Forget it." Sighing, she was looking toward the road when he asked,

"What do you do?"

"Me?" she said. "I'm a tour guide."

John appeared not to have detected her sarcasm; neither did he notice her manifest agitation. "Where's your tour group?" he said. "Did they enjoy *the famous California Redwood Forest?*" He had again sounded like an announcer. Nessa said,

"Loved it. But they had to leave early, the poor fellows." She was still scanning the approaches to the park as she spoke. It was as if she were waiting for someone she knew would never show up. There wasn't another soul in sight. She started to fidget, and John failed to notice this too.

"Maybe you want to give me a little tour before it gets dark?" he said.

"Sure," said she. "If you give me a ride into town."

John said, "A quid pro quo."

No shit, said Nessa's face.

As luck would have it, John could not read her face—or anyone else's. He said, "Ma said not to pick up hitchhikers," and Nessa was already looking incensed by the time he added, "but since you work here, I don't think she would mind." She said,

"That's great."

"After you tell me your name," said John, "we have a deal." She seemed satisfied with this arrangement.

Nessa had changed into another long-sleeve blouse—she always wore long sleeves—and she and John were walking about the park grounds. She said to him after blowing her nose, "You don't look like you're from around here," and she rolled her eyes when he told her,

"No one *is* from around here. I'm on a road trip to one hundred places." She said,

"You think you're funny. Don't you?"

21

He said, "I couldn't tell you." Taking out of his backpack the book Lily gave him, he flashed it in front of Nessa for two seconds before putting it back.

"Can I see it?" she said. "I'm not going to steal it. You know?" She squinted and turned her head to the side. Did she recognize a certain kind of fear in him? "Please?" she said when John didn't comply.

"Okay." He handed the book over. "But I need it back."

Nessa looked at the book's front and back covers. As she leafed through its interior, she nodded to herself and made a face that seemed to say, Could be fun. "You're going to all of them?" she asked. He nodded, and when she said, "It'll take a long time," his answer was,

"I don't care."

Nessa frowned. Taken aback at John's apparent rudeness, she thought, Oh, well, and said, "I see you've been to—wait. You're not following... How do you? They're all over the map, these places. And what are these marks here?" She was referring to the Post-it notes. "You've already gone to..." She was scratching her head. "But the next place is on the opposite coast. You are—"

"Give me back my book," said John.

"You must be spending tons of money." She was handing the book over. "What order are you doing them in?" John seemed confused momentarily as he was replacing the book in his backpack. He said,

"I'm following the book."

"I know you are."

"No," he said. "I really *am* following it."

"You're doing them alphabetically?" She opened her eyes wide in disbelief when he added,

"That's how they're listed. Aren't they?"

They arrived back at the park's trailhead a half-hour later. John was saying, "Maybe I'll go see him anyway, but only after I complete the whole trip."

22

ONE HUNDRED PLACES

"Where is it you said he lives?" she said. "California. Didn't you say?" John said,

"In San Luis Obispo," and after a brief pause, "That's between LA and San Francisco, in the great state of California."

"Cali is exactly where we are," said Nessa. "Why not go see him now? And thanks so much for the geography lesson by the way." He was staring at her.

"Because I want to do it at the end," he said, "after I see the last place. That's why. You're so demanding. Why do you ask so many questions? Are you a reporter or something?"

She said, "Not anymore. But, as a matter of fact, I did go to journalism school for a while." A sigh. "To be the next Barbara Walters." She seemed sad suddenly. "At least, that's what the dream had been all about." She seemed lost in thought for several moments, then said, "I was planning to head east myself." John said,

"You dropped out? Why didn't you finish?"

"That's none of your business," said Nessa, and he did not seem the least bit bothered by her words or by the acridity of her tone. "What are you looking at? Never seen a woman's breasts before?" John kept staring. At first, it seemed as if he were looking at her; at her chest area specifically, for that was the general direction his eyes were pointed in. Or was he seeing *through* her, without seeing her actually? It was as if she were not right there, in front of him. "Fine," she said. "You can look all you want." She paused briefly. "But it's gonna cost you."

"How much?" he said without hesitation.

She slapped him. She slapped him so hard, that she surprised herself. John was reeling back, saying as he went,

"Why did you do that?" Funnily enough, he did not sound at all upset two seconds later as he said, "I can pay you. You know? I have money." When Nessa seemed confused, he said, "Quid pro quo. Remember?"

23

"I don't want your mon—" She arrested that train of thought and made one of those weird faces some people make when they, perhaps thinking it looks 'oh, so sexy,' bite their bottom lip. "You do owe me a ride." Just like that, the earlier version of her reappeared. "You really don't have any?" she said.

John was staring.

"Hey," she said. "I'm talking to you."

"What?" he said.

"The smack, dude."

"Is smack like lysergic acid diethylamide?" He, apparently, could do this without much effort. It was as if the stuff he regurgitated were written right in front of him. She said, "You mean LSD."

John said, "That one really messes you up. It can cause you to hallucinate, feel drunk even, and all without you consuming any alcohol. However, some studies show that the way people experience this drug has a lot to do with their own expectations."

"Oh, really?" she said. She appeared to have spoken only to break the monotony of John' droning on.

He said, "Do you know what else they say?" She negated with her head. "That LSD should not be used as medicine." Her shoulders rose and fell as she sighed. She perked up when John said, "Do you want to come with me?" Looking sweaty and in need of proper rest, she at first seemed reluctant to accept the offer. But then she looked about her. It was getting dark.

"Okay," she said. "I'll come with you." She blew her nose. "I must be getting a cold." She was not.

It was just after sunset, and John was opening the car door for Nessa. There was a hint of military bearing to the way he stood aside. Perhaps a self-taught way of behaving around people of the opposite sex. Or was it something Lily had taught him?

24

ONE HUNDRED PLACES

"Well. Thank you, sir," Nessa said as she curtseyed in front of him. Once she had settled into the passenger seat, John closed the door and went around the back of the car to the other side.

He was fastening his seatbelt when he looked at the Post-it notes on the glove compartment, right in front of Nessa. One of them read: No hitchhikers! Squinting, he scratched his temple momentarily. He said to Nessa, "Fasten your seatbelt."

She told him, "I'm okay," and he told her,

"You must fasten your seatbelt if you want to come with me."

"Yes, sir!" she said. Turning to grab the seatbelt, she looked out of the corner of her eye. John was reaching toward the glove compartment.

He put the Post-it note in his pocket and drove off.

The entrance to Redwood Forest National Park disappeared behind the Oldsmobile.

PART II

Late that evening, John sat waiting in the car, which was parked in front of a highway quick stop. Nessa approached ten minutes later, shopping bag in hand. She got in the car and threw the bag on the back seat. It landed in between John's backpack and hers.

John was minding the road as he drove the following day. Sitting next to him in the passenger seat, Nessa was taking in the Oldsmobile's interior. At one point, she looked in the door map-pocket, which was empty except for a roll of toilet paper. There were several disposable cameras in the glove compartment, as well as a flashlight, stacks of Post-it notes, pens, and some gum. She closed the glove compartment and sat quietly for a moment, bored out of her mind. She reached toward the back seat for her backpack a few moments later and fished out a small purse. Using the mirror on the back of the car's sun visor, she looked at herself as she put on lipstick. She placed the purse inside the map-pocket after she finished, then she reached toward the car's radio.

"Can I?" she said, her hand stopping within inches of the radio. John said,

"Turn it on? I don't know. Can you? Never seen you do it before."

ONE HUNDRED PLACES

Smart ass, thought Nessa. "I was asking permission."

"Then the answer is yes."

An NPR newscast was playing on the radio when Nessa turned it on. Rotating the dial, she searched until she found a station that was playing music. She raised the volume. Her back had not touched the seat backrest when John reached for the radio. He said after lowering the volume,

"I detest loud noises."

"You must mean sounds," said she.

"You understood me."

It was several hours later. John was driving on a multi-lane highway. Nessa was tapping a hand on her thigh in time with the beat of the music. She hummed along to Marc Anthony's "How Could I." John looked at his list of frequencies and said,

"Where do I drop you off?" He reached toward the radio and tuned it back to one of the NPR stations on his list. The news panel game show *Wait Wait... Don't Tell Me!* was on. Stopping in her tracks, Nessa moved her head from side to side. She was scowling at him. She leaned back on the seat and stayed quiet for several moments, the boredom consuming her. After a while, she shifted her body away from John and stared out her window.

John looked rather unhappy as he drove the following afternoon. "Where is it that you get off?" he said.

"It's bright as shit out here," said Nessa. "Got any shades? Where's here anyway?"

"We're driving northeast on route one ninety-nine," he said, "also known as Redwood Highway twenty-five. The closest city is Crescent City, which is twenty-two miles behind us now." After giving him an Are-you-serious? look, Nessa reached behind her for her shopping bag, the contents of which spilled all over the seat.

Toilet paper.

Bottles of water.

Gum.

Crackers.

She was grabbing one of the bottles of water when John said, "Tell me where you're going. I don't have any sunglasses." She faced forward on her seat. "But Ma keeps an old sun visor in there." He was gesturing with his head, indicating the glove compartment, which she opened. As she rummaged through it, she said,

"Why the rush to get rid of me?" Referring to the visor, she added, "No such thing in here."

"Ma would call that a man-look. Try again?" He waited briefly, then said, "Back at the park, you asked me for a ride. I never said you could come with me on my road trip."

Nessa said, "As a matter of fact, you did." She dug in the glove compartment a few more moments and pulled out a visor. It was one of those cheap ones that are decorated with flowers and cats. She inspected it curiously before reaching into the glove compartment once again. "But in case I imagined it... John, can I come on your road trip?" Of the visor, she said, "It's so nice."

"You must mean *may*," John said, and she made a face. He did not appear to have caught her sarcasm regarding the visor.

"What's this?" Nessa said.

"She—Ma loved that visor." When he snatched the piece of paper she was holding, she said,

"Can we pull over? That's a traffic ticket. Isn't it? You got tick—"

"As you like to say," he said. "None of your business. Why do we need to stop? Are you getting off?"

"Because I need to give my hemorrhoids a break," Nessa said, and John looked disgusted the instant she uttered the antepenultimate word. Stifling a yawn, she said, "I need a damn smoke. That's why."

ONE HUNDRED PLACES

He looked at her cigarette. "Why smoke? And why swear so much? Ma said that only ugly people use ugly words." She was glaring at him. "I'll let you come on my road trip, Nessa, but you must be nice."

"I smoke because I can," she said. "Jesus!" Catching herself, she said, "Sorry. Just pull over, dude. Will you?" John started to pull over.

"Where are the headquarters for the tour guides anyway?" he said, but Nessa did not hear him. Already out the door, she was rushing into the bushes, a roll of toilet paper in hand. John stayed put.

Nessa came back twenty minutes later looking all sweaty. She leaned against the front fender of the Oldsmobile and took a couple of drags from her cigarette. She was going for a third when a wince made her stop midway. She grabbed at her belly and cursed to herself as she doubled up. John got out of the car. He was about to say something when she ran back into the bushes.

It was about a week later. John had driven for several hours along OR-62E and US-97N. Merging onto US-20E, he followed it to I-84E.

Nessa was lost in her thoughts as they entered Idaho. John, for his part, seemed lost in a world of his own making as he tapped unconcernedly on the steering wheel. He looked at the road ahead and smiled. In front of him, the afternoon sun had thrown Yellowstone National Park into relief.

The mountains cast shadows over the road as the Oldsmobile entered Yellowstone forty minutes later. Slowing down just enough to reach for his book, John marked the place off with a pen and stuck a Post-it note onto the page before placing the book back on the dashboard.

"Hey," Nessa said when he sped up. John did not appear to have heard her. "Hey! What are you doing?"

"I'm driving," he said.

"Aren't you going to stop?"

He said, "I checked it off already. I don't have to stop to say I've been here."

Nessa tried not to let the true extent of her anger show when she said, "Why. Oh, why. Jesus, dude. We need to check this shit out!" When John just kept going, she felt an urgent need to choke him.

Few other vehicles shared the road with John as he drove through the heart of Yellowstone.

"I need to pee," Nessa said.

"There's a rest-stop eleven point nine miles ahead," said John.

"I need to pee right now."

He ignored her.

"No problem." She shifted her body on her seat. "I can just piss in your mom's car. Is that what you want?"

The car was parked on the side of the road.

Standing behind it, John was transferring wads of bills from the briefcase into his backpack.

Nessa stood by her door. She was squeezing her knees together. "Could you hurry up?"

John hid the briefcase under the suitcase and crossed to the driver-side door. He threw the backpack on the rear seat and moved to the front of the car.

He was already leaning against the hood and looking away from her by the time Nessa slammed the trunk lid shut. She could see the back of his head through the windshield as she crouched behind the car. The lights of an oncoming vehicle shone in the distance.

"Are you almost done?" John said seconds later, the gold tint of the sunset turning his pale complexion several shades darker.

ONE HUNDRED PLACES

"Jesus Christ, John. Shut the hell up. I can't pee with you talking to me."

Turning around, John looked over the roof toward the back of the car, and when his gaze drifted down to the windshield, their eyes met. "Sorry," he said.

"God dammit, John. Don't look." She wrinkled her nose. "What's that awful smell?" She was sniffing the air.

"It's not you," John said, and she rolled her eyes. "We're on the largest geyser field in the world. There are more than ten thousand of them right here. You know?"

"Which doesn't answer my question."

John said, "Ah. You're talking about the aroma of rotten eggs? The favorite dish of the local bacteria is the sulfur in the mud. When they eat it, they make sulfuric acid, which becomes hydrogen sulfide when it turns into a gas and evaporates." She was glaring at him. "It's hydrogen sulfide you're smelling," he said finally.

"You could've started with that."

A crow landed in front of the car, a few feet from John. Cocking its head, the bird cawed as it looked at him. He said, "Guess what just landed here."

"Don't tell me," Nessa said. "An airplane?"

"No." He giggled. "A bird."

Big deal, she thought.

"A crow," John said. "Did you know that crows have a bad reputation? All because they tend to eat crops."

An eighteen-wheeler slowed down somewhat as it drove past the Oldsmobile. It was going in the opposite direction John and Nessa were traveling.

Nessa was startled when the driver—he had glanced in her direction—honked.

John looked over his shoulders; this time, however, he raised a hand and sort of tried to cover his eyes.

"I swear," Nessa said. "Turn around one more time, and I'll break your fucking knee caps."

He turned his head forward again and observed the crow a few moments. "In all actuality," he said, "their abilities rival that of chimps, you know? Scientists even believe they possess foresight."

Nessa came to stand next to him at the front of the car a moment later, and the crow hopped toward her. She scared it away. As the bird flew away, John seemed fascinated by it. His brow furrowed a tad. He perked up for some reason. Watching him, Nessa thought there was something that seemed different about John. It was as if, somehow, the encounter with the bird had started a wheel turning inside his head.

The following day, as John drove on a road lined with pines and fir trees, Nessa took hold of his book. She turned it over in her hands and, after giving it a quick flip-through, waved it toward John.

"Why?" she said.

"Why what?" said John.

"This trip, why the heck are you doing it?" She was waiting for an answer. He didn't give one. "You're running away from a girlfriend or something?"

"No," he said, adding matter-of-factly, "My Ma died. I left."

"Shit. I'm sorry," she said.

"It's okay," said John. "She had cancer."

Which didn't make Nessa feel any better.

"It metastasized into her blood stream," John said, "and transferred the cancer cells into her brain, where it grew for two years forty-nine days and fourteen hours until it cut off brain functions around her medulla oblongata."

TMI, thought Nessa. "But you're not doing it just because. Are you?"

He said, "I think she was afraid I'd never venture outside of our hometown." He paused awhile. "It's weird. She never ordered me around or anything like that." He glanced in her direction. "Don't look at me like that. I'm sure she didn't do it for my sake only."

"Oh, no?" Nessa said.

"No. She was a gentle soul with everyone she met."

Hearing this made her feel sad—until he said,

"Can we stop talking about Ma for a while?"

Quite taken aback at his abruptness, she said only, "Okay."

A few hours later, they stopped for food and gas. They then followed I-80E to Oregon, where they spent the night.

Nessa drove through Utah the following day; then John drove almost straight through Wyoming. Staying on I-80E, he headed toward Nebraska. "Don't you have any other relatives beside that uncle of yours?" Nessa said.

John was shaking his head from side to side. "Only my mother's brother. He's situated somewhere in the outskirts of San Luis Obispo."

"You told me that already," she said after a yawn the size of Tasmania.

John said, "Why do you ask, then?" and he added before she could answer, "I only told you he was my uncle. Could he have been my father's brother?"

She yawned once again, thinking all the while, Smart ass. As she rolled her eyes, John asked,

"Why do you yawn so much?"

"Don't tell me I need a reason for that too," she said. "God. You make me feel so dumb."

"Is that so?" he said. "I shouldn't be able to hold that much sway over the way you feel. If you feel dumb, you probably are."

Choosing to ignore this latter comment, Nessa said, "Why not go see him? Might be bet—"

"Because he's not a nice man," he said cutting her off.

Nessa was saying, "So, you don't even have a place to li—?" when she stopped herself. "People change. You know?"

33

"Is that what happened to you?" said John. "Did you change for the worse, or have you always been addicted to drugs?"

She was about to speak, but once again he cut her off.

"Are you going to change once more, *stop using*, as they say in your circles?"

She sucked air into her lungs and blew it out slowly through her mouth as he said,

"I had my mom's house to live in until uncle Bonnie bought it from me."

Nessa said, "Why would he do that?"

"He said I didn't need it," said John. "And I agree with that assertion as matter of fact." Now he picked up the thread of their other topic. "Not everyone wants to change. You know? Some of us can't."

Feeling sorry for him, she replaced the book on the dashboard. John said,

"Ma said she bought me that book for a reason."

"Don't worry," she said. "I'll make sure you don't let her down." Uncomfortable at the extended silence that followed, she broke it by saying, "So, are we just gonna keep driving from one place to the next following your book until we hit a hundred?" John was scratching his head. "I'm sure you realize that these locations are all over the map. It'd be much more economical if we went in a circle or something, and a lot faster."

"I don't need to rush," John said.

It was not the answer she had expected.

John said, "I had never taken a vacation. Hadn't even left my hometown before this trip."

Weird, she thought.

"So," said John, "if I get to see all one hundred places, it doesn't matter to me how long it takes."

She said, "Sounds like that's all you want out of life."

"Exactly," said John. "I could die afterward."

"Oh. Don't be so tragic," Nessa said chuckling.

ONE HUNDRED PLACES

"It's the truth."

"Okay," she said, and he told her,

"But you can leave whenever you want."

She was about to say something nastier, but she refrained. "You have two problems, John." He looked at her. "You're crazy, and you think you're funny."

"Ma thought I was."

"What?" she said. "Crazy?"

John said, "What do you think?"

She was giggling as they entered Nevada.

As they passed through Iowa, John stopped only for gas and a quick bite. It was night by the time they arrived in Illinois. The Oldsmobile was parked on the street in a shabby, squalid area of Aurora. Nessa exited the car. She had shut the door and was taking off toward a street corner when John yelled from inside the car,

"Ma always said drugs make you stupid."

She stepped back toward the car and stuck her head in thorough the front passenger window. "And what's your excuse?"

John gulped. "You're not being nice, Nessa."

She told him, "Just wait here."

"Tell me where you're going," he said.

"Be right back," was all she said before hurrying away and turning around the corner.

John turned the radio on and found it tuned to the last station Nessa had been listening to. As he waited, Madonna's 'Express Yourself' and Depeche Mode's 'Master and Servant,' came on.

John was still fidgeting in his seat forty-five minutes later. Suddenly he started removing the Post-it notes off the dashboard. When he was finished, he ripped them in half, then ripped them again. He threw the torn pieces of paper out the window and turned the radio off before pushing his

35

back against his seat. Closing his eyes, he began to take deep breaths. He stayed like this for several moments before exiting the car, and only after he had picked up every single piece of paper off the pavement, did he march to the corner around which Nessa had disappeared.

The alleyway looked grim, forbidding, in the semi-darkness. John took in as much of it as the light would allow. Several homeless people lay on the sidewalk. One of them, a woman in her twenties, was reclining against a wall, ready to fall. John stopped to stare at her for a few moments, after which he looked behind him and continued down this corridor of misery.

"Give me more. I want more."

The voice, though slurred, sounded a lot like Nessa's. John followed it into a drug-dealing joint.

Filthy and unsavory, the place reeked of urine. Used syringes lay on the floor in front of a cot which occupied a corner of the room.

On the cot was Nessa, high as a kite. She was drifting in and out of consciousness as she repeated in a monotone, "I want more, now. Give it to me again." She did not react when John said,

"There you are." He was digging for the pieces of paper in his pocket and throwing them into the already-full, medium-size trash can at the foot of the cot. As he went to cross to Nessa's side, an arm halted his advance.

"Where're you going, Bro?" said a man in his thirties, the drug dealer in charge of the joint.

John pointed at Nessa. "I'm going to get her."

"Hell, you are," the dealer said. "What's she to you?" By this time, two other thugs in their late twenties had just surrounded John, who was saying,

"She's my friend."

"She's *my* friend now," said the dealer.

ONE HUNDRED PLACES

It was not clear whether John understood the implications this statement carried. He said, "She's your friend, too? She must have a lot of friends." When he reached for the dealer's arm, one of the thugs hit him in the rib cage. The other head-butted him in the face. John doubled down. Bleeding and looking dazed, he grabbed at his mouth as he went to stand straight. That's when the first thug kicked him behind the knees. He lost his balance and landed on the floor, where both thugs proceeded to kick him in the head and rib cage until the dealer gestured at them: Stop.

Nessa was barely able to stand on her own as John, his face bruised and bleeding, steered her out of the drug-dealing joint. He was wincing in pain as he was laboring up the alleyway with her in tow. He stopped to look back every other minute as if he were afraid the two thugs were going to come after him.

John stooped down and laid Nessa on the backseat of the Oldsmobile. Her body had gone limp. Grimacing in pain, he got behind the wheel, but the car did not start when he turned the key, and he started slamming his fist against the steering wheel. He caught himself and looked toward the backseat. Nessa was still passed out. A muted clank filled the silence seconds later as John pulled on the hood release. He reached toward the glove compartment.

A beam of light from a torch illuminated the engine compartment of the Oldsmobile. John was fiddling with the battery. Taking the flashlight, he hammered the top of the clamps on the battery terminal and, after making sure they were seated properly, reached in through the driver-side window and turned the key in the ignition.

The engine barely turned.

He kicked his foot one time against the car door before coming back for the flashlight and slamming the hood shut, after which he rushed toward the corner. He had already turned into the alleyway when he stopped suddenly and turned around. Returning to the car, he opened the driver-side door and reached under the dashboard. The trunk popped open.

"I can't believe this. You didn't get enough?"

John was standing on the threshold of the door of the drug-dealing joint. He didn't look scared, but he didn't look too comfortable in his skin either. He said to the dealer, "I need help."

"What kind of help?" said the leader as the two thugs who had beaten the shit out of John appeared behind him. They squeezed past John and stood outside the door behind him.

"My car won't start."

The dealer scratched his chin a few moments.

"What makes you think I'd want to help?"

A fidgety John swallowed as the two thugs grinned at each other.

A car engine revved several times.

After the drug dealer removed the jumper cables from the battery terminals on the Oldsmobile, the two thugs removed the ones on the battery terminals of the dealer's 2009 Chrysler Sebring, which was facing John's car.

John exited the Oldsmobile and went to retrieve the jumper cables from the two thugs. They looked at each other as he stood in front of them, his hand extended in front of him.

The drug dealer took John's flashlight from where it had been placed in the engine compartment of the Oldsmobile. He slammed the hood shut and spent some time peering into the car through the windshield.

"Aren't you gonna say Thanks, at least?" he said pointing the flashlight in John's direction. Although the light was shining down toward his chest rather than his face, John squinted as he said,

38

"Thank you."

The dealer bit his lower lip repeatedly. He was looking at John sort of funny. "You may wanna put those away."

"These?" John looked at the jumper cables he was holding. "It's okay," he said. "They're not heavy." The two thugs looked at each other as if dumbfounded. The dealer signaled with his head, at them, and as they were moving toward the back of the Oldsmobile, he crossed to its open driver-side door. He reached in and popped open the trunk. John said,

"What do you want?" He was following the dealer to the rear of the Oldsmobile. The dealer said,

"Just checking things out. You know?"

"Oh," said John, and the dealer said,

"You don't mind. Do you?"

John negated with his head and went to put the jumper cables in the trunk.

"Stop," the dealer said.

John froze. The two thugs surrounded him.

The dealer was pointing the flashlight toward the trunk. All he could see was the large suitcase, which occupied most of the trunk's real estate. It lay open in there, half of John´s clothes strewn all around it. Making a face at what he must have perceived as untidiness, the dealer turned around. "Here," he said, and he handed John the flashlight before signaling with his head at his two minions.

John had thrown the jumper cables in the trunk and was reaching up to close it when the dealer crossed toward his car, the two thugs trailing him.

The latter group was already in the car. It seemed they were ready to go. John got behind the wheel of the Oldsmobile and was closing his door when the drug dealer exited from his car. He was coming back toward the Oldsmobile. John stiffened.

The dealer passed by John´s side and stopped in front of the rear door. He peered through the window. Nessa was still passed out on the back seat. Opening the door, the dealer hovered over her as he looked around back there. But nothing seemed to jump at him. Nothing except for some left-over food items and a few empty plastic bottles on the floor of the car. And John's backpack under Nessa's head. He scratched the side of his face as he turned his head and looked toward his car through the Oldsmobile's windshield. He must have thought that the backpack had been filled with clothes so that it could be used as a pillow, for he withdrew. Pushing the door closed, he didn't even look in John's direction when he passed by him on the way back to his own car.

John waited for the drug dealer to drive away, then he got back on the road himself.

Nessa stirred in her sleep about three hours later. She looked about her, disoriented, as she woke up. Yep, she was in the back seat of a car.

The Oldsmobile was parked in front of a highway quick-stop.

She sat up, and as she looked toward the front of the car, she saw John through the windshield. He was scanning the shelves inside the store.

John trudged out moments later carrying a small brown bag. "You're awake," he said.

"No. I'm not," said Nessa. She looked from side to side out the back windows. "Where are we?" Ignoring the question, John got in and started the car. "Do you want to take me to bed?" Nessa said as he drove away.

John told her, "That's the plan."

Nessa let him drive around in the small town for about twenty minutes before saying to him, "What are you doing?"

He said, "I'm looking for a motel."

Nessa said, "Let's just do it right here."

ONE HUNDRED PLACES

Apparently, John didn't get what she was intimating, for he said, "Not in the car. I want to sleep in a proper bed tonight."

"Sleep?" Nessa's index finger 'shot' her through the temple and she fell sideways on the seat.

They had stopped at a small roadside motel in Perú, Illinois, and she was trying to pull John toward the bed.

"Please, John. Please." He was resisting. "You're sick. You need medicine."

"I'm not sick," she said. "I'm just hot." He felt her forehead.

"Yes. You are."

"Then...?"

He reached into the brown bag. "You may have a fever." He poured a cupful of sleep syrup and offered it to her.

She said, "That's no—"

"Take it," said John. "You'll feel better."

"I won't drink that."

"Take it," he said. "Then we'll go to bed."

"You promise?"

He nodded.

"Okay," she said, and gulped the whole thing.

John took the cup from her hand. "One more."

She started to say, "One is enou—"

"Ma always gave me two." He refilled the cup, handed it to her.

"Okay, doctor," she said before emptying the second cup. John said,

"Now, lie in bed. I'll take a shower. Okay?"

She nodded, and as he was crossing toward the bathroom, a fleeting moment of lucidity assailed her. She felt vulnerable. And then the feeling was gone.

John stopped on the threshold of the bathroom door. He turned only his head as he looked at her. Her eyes were bathing him in lust. "Get in bed," he said.

41

Nessa kept her eyes on him as she complied.

John was running warm water over his wounds. As he did, blood streamed down the side of his face from around the left temple. It splashed onto the bathroom sink. With blood oozing also from his nose and lips, he buried his face in a towel for a few moments. After he had wrung the blood-stained cloth under the tap, he hung it on the shower rod before coming back to the sink, where he looked in the mirror.

There was a large hematoma on his forehead, smaller ones on his lips. A rivulet of blood still ran down his temple. Blood dripped from his nose when he stooped down to grab some toilet paper, and he winced as he straightened back up. Pressing the palm of his hand over his ribcage caused him to wince once again. He rolled some of the toilet paper and put it in his nostrils; with the rest, he dabbed at the cuts in his face.

He pulled the bathroom door closed behind him as he came back into the bedroom. Nearing the bed, he leaned over it and looked at Nessa. She was snoring. The bottle of sleep syrup was in her night table; the measuring cup, in her hand.

John retrieved the cup and tiptoed to his side of the bed. After putting everything in the drawer, he turned off the lights.

Morning light filtered in from around the edges of the window curtains as the sound of running water drifted into the bedroom. Nessa stirred in bed as the sound stopped.

John came in from the bathroom several moments later. Already dressed in different clothes from what he had been wearing the night before, he was dabbing at his nose with a piece of paper as he looked toward the bed. Nessa was still asleep.

ONE HUNDRED PLACES

Opening the front door, John fiddled with its locking mechanism a few moments, turning the handle a few times from inside.

Probably thinking he had it all figured out, he went out onto the balcony and pulled the door closed without making any noise.

He was still leaning on the balcony railing about an hour later, the sun on his face, which was swollen and purple in places. He looked sort of relaxed as he ambled back to the room door and turned the handle.

The door didn't open. He tried again, and again, but got the same result: every time, the handle would shift down, but it would not engage the electronic lock.

John had made a fist as he was lifting his arm; however, it was the palm of his hand which hit on the door lightly.

Oh well, his face seemed to say. Shrugging, he crossed back toward the balustrade of the balcony.

Nessa scanned the room as she woke up. Immediately, she became confused. Waking up in a different place every day made it necessary for her to take several moments to ascertain her whereabouts. She knew that neither her mental state nor the splitting headache she had just then would help her situation. She squeezed her eyes shut and called out, "John?" She opened her eyes. "John?" Leaping off the bed, she rushed to the bathroom. Knock, knock. "John. Are you in there?" She knocked a few more times before turning the handle and pushing open the door. A peculiar pang of panic, of a sort she wasn't prone to experiencing, invaded her as she stepped into the empty bathroom.

John's lips looked dry as he stood on the second-floor balcony of the motel. Squinting at the brightness of the midday sun, he scratched his head as he paced up and down

43

the length of the balcony. He ran smack into Nessa when she rushed out of their room. "Nessa!"

He sounded all excited.

Nessa thought he looked genuinely happy to see her. With her heart beating at faster than its normal rate, she pressed her lips together and breathed through her nose momentarily. What a relief.

"There you are," she said. "I thought you had—what's wrong with your face?" she said when she noticed the state of John's face.

He said, "You thought I'd left you."

"I'm hungry," said she.

"You don't remember?" he said.

She tried to remember. She couldn't; the memories of the night before were lost in the general fog that clouded her mind.

"You're hungry too?" she said when John pressed a hand on his ribcage. He followed her when she turned back toward the room, and as soon as there was enough space for him to pass her, he hurried toward the bathroom. "Seriously," she said standing in the middle of the room. "What happened to your face?"

"I must have fallen or something," said John. "You really don't remember. Do you?"

"Am I supposed to remember something?"

The sound of John slurping water drifted into the room. It stopped just before he said, "Nothing really. I went to bed last night and woke up with this face." As Nessa shook her head from side to side, he added, "And, apparently, one or two broken ribs too."

She waited for the slurping to return. "That's not funny, John. Just tell me what happened. Okay?"

"Okay," John said. He came back into the bedroom. "If you insist." He sat on the edge of the bed. "This is what happened…"

ONE HUNDRED PLACES

Evelyn, a fifty-six-year-old, young-at-heart redhead took a long drag of her cigarette as she scanned the faces of her dozen or so customers from behind the counter. Across from her, on the other side of the counter, was John. He was browsing the extensive menu of the roadside-restaurant as Nessa, perched on the stool next to his, leg crossed and tucked under her, rested her chin in her cupped hands. Minutes later, after Nessa had already ordered two hot dogs and an apple pie, John looked up from his menu. He was about to speak when Evelyn said to him,

"What happened to your face?"

"She hit me," John said with a straight face.

Nessa couldn't tell, from the way Evelyn was looking at her, whether the waitress believed John. Setting her eyes on her menu once again, she made herself not laugh aloud as John started to order his food.

"I want the Mother's Chicken Fried Steak," he said. As Evelyn took the order, he went back to examining the menu, and he didn't even look back at her when he next spoke. "How did you get Ma's recipe?" he said. "She never served it with peas. Also, the onion gravy goes on the side, not on top of the mashed potatoes."

A quiet, annoyed sigh issued from Evelyn, and she rolled her eyes and clicked her pen as she waited for him to continue. "Yes," he said. "I'll have the Mother's Chicken Fried Steak with the mashed potatoes and the onion gravy and the peas with butter; and I want everything on a separate plate so I can put it all together the right way." Evelyn said to him,

"Really? You're kidding me."

"Yes," said John. "No—I mean, no. I want the 'Mother's Chicken Fried Steak' on one plate, the peas on a separate plate, the mashed potatoes on another plate, and the gravy on another."

Evelyn was about to interject, but he didn't give her the chance. "Also," he said, "the butter for the peas must be on another plate." Evelyn finished committing everything to her notepad before turning to go, at which time John said, "Make sure the gravy isn't cold." He had spoken loud enough that every other guest in the restaurant turned to look at him.

Nessa wanted to disappear underneath the counter. She mouthed an 'I'm sorry' at Evelyn, who had sent a quick glance in her direction before storming toward the kitchen.

It was about forty-five minutes later. John was using separate silverware to combine the different parts of his meal. As he did, he whispered to Nessa, "Ma didn't use so much breading."

"Just eat up, will you?" she said scowling at him.

Beyond the counter, Evelyn once again was watching her guests from behind another cigarette. It seemed she didn't hear Nessa and John's exchange.

Nessa ate like there was no tomorrow while John took his time with his food.

As Evelyn was cleaning up the table, she glanced toward the front of the restaurant. John and Nessa, who were visible through a window, were getting in the Oldsmobile. A napkin with writing on it was on the counter, next to the empty plates. Evelyn grabbed it, and a one-hundred-dollar bill fell out of it. It landed on the floor, where Evelyn stooped down to get it. She read the hand-written note on the napkin.

Sorry my friend put you through all that shit, Nessa had written. Hope this makes up for it. The note ended with a hand-drawn smiley face.

Astonished, Evelyn ran to the threshold of the restaurant kitchen door. "You shouldn't have spat on those peas!" she whispered to her redheaded husband-cook, who was facing away from her.

ONE HUNDRED PLACES

All he did was shrug.

John got back on the highway and headed east toward Chicago. There was a look of satisfaction in his face as he patted his stomach. Nessa said, "You know. You can't go on behaving like that around people."

"No?" John said.

"You need to learn to act like a normal human being sometimes."

"Like a normal human being? What is that?"

She said, "Can you at least try to remember a few basic things?"

"This is how I am, Nessa."

"And you can't change that," she said, "but you can't go around hurting people's feelings at every turn either."

"What about at every other?" He was grinning.

"Can you be serious for a minute?" She was quiet awhile. "I know," she said. "I've got an idea." She noticed John's furrowed brow. "We're gonna put one of your obsessions to good use."

John blinked a few times when he looked in the interior rear-view mirror. Then his eyes opened wide. The sound of a siren was heard in the distance. A highway patrol car, its lights flashing, was closing in on the Oldsmobile. Panic washed over John, and he began to fidget as the sound of the siren got closer.

Nessa heard the siren just as the Oldsmobile swerved left. John had taken his hands off the steering wheel and was covering his ears.

Reacting just in time, Nessa reached sideways and took control of the wheel. She saw the police car in the rear-view mirror. "It's probably a traffic stop." She was almost certain John didn't hear it when she then said, "Calm down."

He was staring straight ahead and seemingly lost in some distant memory.

PEDRO VASQUEZ

John and Lily had been at home having dinner, and she was telling him, "Don't get stopped by the police when you go out of town, hon."

John took back control of the steering wheel, and instead of pulling over, stepped on the gas.

"What are you doing!" Nessa said frightened.

"Ma said not to stop. I can't stop."

She began to stroke his shoulder—like Lily used to. It looked as if John had stopped breathing. "It's okay, hon," she told him. "Just pull over, okay?"

John looked at her an instant and let out a deep sigh.

The Oldsmobile was stopped on the side of the road. A police officer came up to the driver-side door and hit the window with his baton.

Knock, knock.

In his mid-fifties, Ray looked like mischief became him. He was sliding his glasses halfway down his nose with his index finger.

John squirmed in his seat as Ray fixed his eyes on him. The last time he had looked half as nervous had been during the weeks—more than a decade ago—he spent taking and retaking his driving test.

"For a minute there," Ray said, "I thought we were gonna have ourselves a little chase."

All John could say was, "I—I."

Ray said, "Did you know your left brake-light is out?" John negated with his head. "License and registration please."

Nessa wanted to appear calm, but she was freaking out inside.

"I—out?" John said. He was driving without a proper license of course. "The ground wire fell off again?" he said. "A twelve-volt light bulb. I can—I can fix that—fix it myself, I can. Heck. I can fix anything."

"Shh," Nessa said in a whisper. "Shut up a bit."

ONE HUNDRED PLACES

Ray said to her, "Please, ma'am, let the gentleman finish." Looking down at John, the police officer smirked. He tapped the baton against the palm of his hand a few times before saying, "So, you know about electricity, and cars, and all that, son?"

As John nodded, Nessa heard Ray say, almost to himself, "Nice. Very nice."

Ray's police cruiser, lights still flashing, zoomed by on Illinois Route 17 West. Way behind it, was John's Oldsmobile trying to keep up.

Nice! thought Nessa as the two cars drove onto Ray's property, on which a barn stood adjacent to the main house. Ray parked his police cruiser in between the two. John stopped behind him.

Having stayed behind in the Oldsmobile after John exited the car, Nessa had finished putting on lipstick when she saw Ray exit from the police car and cross toward the barn. She was thirsty and wanted to start snooping around in the main house. She started toward it after playfully kicking the door of the Oldsmobile shut, but then she changed direction and followed John, who had followed Ray into the barn.

The structure housed a tractor and other farm equipment in disrepair. Two 1970 Ford Fairlanes sat side by side in a corner, a tarpaulin separating them from the farm equipment. There was nothing in here for her, thought Nessa, and she turned around and headed toward the house.

John slid out from under one of the Fairlanes about one hour later, his hands and the front of his shirt smeared with grease and dirty oil. Searching in a small toolbox Ray had set for him nearby, he found a wrench and slid back under the car.

PEDRO VASQUEZ

Less than two minutes later, Ray exited the main house via a side door. He hurried around the house and came out on the other side, ending up behind John's car. Nearing the side of the Oldsmobile that was farthest from the house, he opened the front passenger door.

Lily's visor and John's book were on the dashboard. Post-it notes stuck out from about one-third of the book's pages. No one was watching when Ray looked behind him, and he got in the car and closed the door. He whistled to himself as he lifted Nessa's purse out of the map-pocket and put it back after having looked inside. He examined the contents of the map pocket some more and peered through the hole of a roll of toilet paper he fished out of it. There was nothing in there. He was about to drop the roll of toilet paper back where he found it, but something caught his attention. Another roll of toilet paper, almost-depleted, lay flat at the bottom of the map-pocket.

After he had maneuvered the roll back into its normal shape, Ray looked through the hole. His fat fingers tried to reach for what he discovered; however, whatever it was, it had been jammed in. He just could not pull it out.

Four small bags of marijuana that were bound together with a rubber band fell onto Ray's lap when he ripped in half the roll of toilet paper.

John slid out from under the car and stretched his back before walking around to the driver-side door. Starting the car, he revved up the engine several times before turning the ignition back off. He turned toward the second Fairlane.

It took him about an hour to finish fiddling with the underside of the second car, and he looked exhausted when he slid out from under it. He lifted the hood and inspected the engine compartment before fixing his attention on the windshield wiper motors.

ONE HUNDRED PLACES

Nessa stood on the threshold of the kitchen door and looked toward the back of the house.

Shelly, Ray's wife, was hovering over the kitchen counter. She was making lemonade. "You guys' been together long?" asked the fifty-year-old woman. "You make a nice couple." As Nessa giggled, Shelly said, "He seems like such a nice man."

"Actually, we met just recently," Nessa said. Shelly looked rather surprised. "But, yes, he's nice enough."

Shelly dried her hands on the apron she was wearing, and got a tray and matching glasses from the cupboard in front of her above the counter. Taking the jug of lemonade, she said to Nessa, "Come on. They must be dead tired, those poor fellows."

Nessa grabbed the tray with the glasses.

John gulped the glass of lemonade Nessa had handed him. "Are you having fun, Nessa?" he said.

"Tons," said she as she scanned the barn. "Where is he?" she whispered. "He's not helping you?" At the other end of the barn, Shelly, jug and glass in hand, was walking behind the tarpaulin.

John said, "Right now, he's doing something other than helping. I think."

Nessa's brow furrowed, and she said, "Oh, really? I wonder what that may be. Let's go see." When she strode after Shelly, John followed. They reached the tarpaulin and ran into Shelly, who was on her way back. She still carried the jug and a glassful of lemonade.

"Oops," Nessa said. "Sorry. We just wanted to check on—" She saw Ray.

Ray was asleep on a reclining chair, a small mask strapped over his nose. A seven-feet-long tube that attached to the mask ran down to a machine which was sitting on a stool next to the recliner.

"He doesn't get enough sleep, the poor man," Shelly said. "His schedule doesn't help." She looked at John. "I'm sure he wanted to help." She sniffed the air. "Does something smell funny in here?"

As Nessa watched John scratch his head, her nose detected the peculiar odor in the air. She couldn't help perking up as she recognized the smell. She tried not to draw attention to herself, but she was becoming nervous.

"A C-PAP machine?" she said. "How neat." Her life had gone to shit the last few years, but she knew there was still a working brain inside that skull of hers—and sometimes it worked. All she needed to do right now was keep her thoughts from affecting her demeanor. "He has sleep apnea," she said to John.

"Sleep apnea?" he said. "I know about that."

Done, thought Nessa. Thank you. She hid a grin; for she knew what was coming.

"Apnea is the name doctors give to any pause in breathing," John said. "They call it hypopnea when the breaths are abnormally low."

As Ray stirred in his sleep, something caught Nessa's attention. Something was sticking out of one of the police officer's pockets.

"It's a very dangerous condition," John said, "because people can stop breathing for whole minutes in the most severe cases."

Ray stirred once again, and the thing that had caught Nessa's attention became evident. She held her breath when a piece of toilet paper fell out of Ray's pocket and hit the ground. Poorly wrapped in the toilet paper, was a bag of marijuana.

"It can happen many times every hour," John was saying. As he continued his impromptu lecture, Nessa realized she was becoming even more nervous. She tried to hide it by casually rubbing her hands together. John said, "There are three types of apneas depending on the underlying cause:

central, obstructive, and mixed. The latter is a combination of the first two, of course. But most people suffer from the obstructive kind." Shelly looked as if she could not believe her ears; her jaw dropped when John continued. "And did you know? When organ donors die in a hospital, doctors disconnect all the machines to produce a brain apnea."

Shelly said, "Really?"

John was nodding as he said, "They do it to make sure that the person is dead indeed."

"Boy," said Shelly, "you sure know your stuff."

"That's enough, John," Nessa said.

Ray woke up and noticed he had an audience.

"I'm sure she knows all about it." Nessa had not noticed Ray yet. "Besides, I don't think that that last bit has anything to do with sleep apnea."

When Ray removed the mask, the noise from the C-PAP machine made Shelly, John, and Nessa turn to face him. The police officer's demeanor was one of resignation when he said, "Sorry you had to see this." Nessa noticed the marks the mask had left along the sides of Ray's face and on his forehead.

John was staring at his feet. Perhaps he was embarrassed to have been caught looking? As Ray set his mask down on the stool, he saw the marijuana on the floor. He glanced at Nessa, who was saying,

"It's okay. My father had the same—" She stopped in her tracks when she noticed Ray's look. She couldn't avoid gulping. "...problem."

"What problem?" John said as Shelly asked Ray,

"Do you notice that smell, love?"

Because of where they had been standing in relation to Ray, neither Shelly nor John had seen the marijuana. Ray said to his wife,

"I don't smell anything." He smirked and was looking at Nessa when he said, "Do you guys?"

"I do," John said, "and it's not a nice smell!"

Nessa shook her head from side to side. She reached for John's elbow. "Come," she said. "Let's finish what you came here to do before it gets dark."

John said, "You're going to help?"

She pushed him along. "You wish."

Shelly was running a hand over her husband's upper back as he was gulping his glassful of lemonade. When he finished the drink, he dried the commissures of his lips with his thumb and index finger. He smiled to himself as he watched Nessa and John go.

It was late afternoon, and the barn was only dimly lit as John worked on the tail-light wiring of the second Ford Fairlane.

Ray climbed behind the wheel several moments later, and John stepped back from the car and stood behind it. The police officer looked in the rear-view mirror. John was taking a hand to his mouth and feeling the scabs of the lesions on his lips. Ray yelled, "Ready?"

"Step on the brakes now," John yelled back. When the red light from the car's brakes reflected on his face and clothing seconds later, he extended both arms and gave two thumbs up.

Night had fallen. Ray was outside fiddling with his police cruiser when Shelly came out of the house. She went to offer a brown bag to John, who was already sitting behind the wheel in the Oldsmobile. "Something for the road," she said.

John seemed ready to go. "Thank you, ma'am," he was saying to Shelly when Nessa got in the car next to him. The Oldsmobile started, and Ray stopped what he was doing. He waved at John and said,

"John, boy. You drive safe now." John had raised his hand and was about to wave back at Ray. He quickly lowered it when the police officer added, "And don't let me catch you driving without a license again."

ONE HUNDRED PLACES

Looking somewhat confused, John turned toward Nessa, who told him, "Don't look at me." She was giggling inside.

"I'm kidding, John," said Ray. "You just be careful out there. Okay, buddy?"

Nessa was giving John a look and a shrug as Ray was laughing an ugly laugh in the background. She put on an insincere Sorry-for-you-my-friend face.

John drove away, and Shelly went to stand at her husband's side. The two of them waved as the Oldsmobile left their property.

Ray's free hand reached into his pocket. He felt the little plastic bag he had in there.

It had been several hours since they had left Ray and Shelly's place, and John looked haggard as he drove. Feigning a yawn, Nessa glanced right and down, at the map pocket. The big roll of toilet-paper was still in there; her purse, too. She looked at John out of the corner of her eye. After she'd made sure he was minding the road, she surreptitiously lifted the roll of toilet paper. A single bag of marijuana, a rubber band, and the torn pieces of cardboard from the other toilet-paper roll remained. She covered her mouth but could not help snickering.

"What is it?" John said.

"Nothing." It was ludicrous, she thought. A so-called officer of the law taking not just one, but three, of her baggies. She was gonna have to get her hands on some more—either that, or the other thing... And she didn't want to have to do that other thing. "Want me to drive?" she said.

"No, Nessa. Thank you."

"Suit yourself," said she.

John said, "Could you please put on your seatbelt?"

"Yes, sir." She had rolled her eyes at John's veiled command, but she was actually smiling inside when she reached for the seatbelt. At first, she thought John was making progress, and when she realized what was happening,

55

she said, "You're such a weirdo." John had been reading from the Post-it notes she had plastered all over the steering wheel of the car—for his sake, she had told herself.

He said, "And you're such a bossy person."

She regarded the notes, which said stuff like: Say thanks. Ask before changing the radio station. Ask me how I'm doing.

"Just trying to help," she said.

"Thanks," John said after reading another of the Post-it notes.

"Ha ha," she said. "Funny guy." She reached into her bag and pulled out her cigarettes. When she lit up, John leaned over and pointed to the Post-it note that was right in front of her on the glove compartment.

The note said, 'No smoking. Love, Mom.'

She felt like telling him off, but she thought better of it and flicked the cigarette out the window.

Weeks later, an attendant was leaning against the open door of the gas station quick stop he got paid minimum wage to slave at. He was chewing some of the cheapest tobacco they sold at 'his store' and staring off into nowhere. The Oldsmobile, with John at the wheel, drove up to the pumps.

"Go pay him," John was saying to Nessa. She didn't had time to react before he added, "No, wait. Can you, please, go pay while I pump the gas?"

Nessa thought, Now, that's progress!

The quick-stop attendant—he wore a trucker hat backward—revealed a couple of missing upper teeth when he smiled. He was checking Nessa out as she approached.

Arcing up as she spoke, Nessa's left hand came across to the other side of her body, index finger pointing backward over her shoulder at the Oldsmobile, when she said, "Fifty bucks for that car."

ONE HUNDRED PLACES

Salaciousness dripped off the attendant's every word when he said to her, "A pretty little thing like you don't have to pay. You know?"

Nessa did a double take. "What did you say?"

"I mean," said the horn dog—as if she didn't understand what he was insinuating. "You leave the faggot behind, meet me behind the building... The gas, as good as paid..."

Nessa slapped him. She slapped him so hard that she felt her palm burn afterward. She threw a fifty-dollar bill at his face and hurried back to the car, where John had about finished filling up. John replaced the fuel nozzle in its holder at once when she told him, "Drive."

The attendant looked stunned. When he reacted at the last moment and began running toward the pumps, they were already driving away. He went after the car anyway.

John looked in the rear-view mirror as the Oldsmobile got back on the road. The attendant was still giving chase. "Did you forget something?" John said glancing at Nessa. "That guy is—"

"Didn't forget anything," she said, and she thought it was priceless the look of confusion in John's face. It prompted her to say, "*He* did. He forgot his manners."

The attendant's fist was pumping the air as he shouted obscenities at the receding Oldsmobile. In between bouts of shouts, he would bend down at the edge of the road and pick up a few stones, which he hurled at the car. However, the car was already out of reach. The improvised projectiles landed on the asphalt, where they rolled several feet before coming to a stop.

John said to Nessa, "You can't continue to behave like that around people. You know?"

"Copycat," she said. "Those are my words."

"And they fit you perfectly," he said. He turned serious before adding, "You're not stupid, Nessa. Don't act stupid."

She was about to say something but changed her mind at the last instant and just sat there watching him.

PEDRO VASQUEZ

A couple and their kid were enjoying a day at the park in Spoon River Valley, Illinois, where the foliage was already dressed in the glorious colors of fall. One of the adults signaled to the other, and the pair got to their feet.

John and Nessa had been following a dirt trail through the park. They were about two minutes away from what would be their closest approach to the spot where the family was picnicking.

The couple came to meet them. The man got in John's way. His wife, bible in hand, had to run to catch up to Nessa, who shook her head at the woman and moved away from her as quickly as she could.

A restroom was located at the far end of the park. Nessa crossed to it and went inside. John took the religious-looking pamphlet the man was offering him. He began to rub his fingers on it. It looked as if he were examining the texture of the paper.

"Did you know," John said to the man, "paper is made by separating and rearranging the fibers from trees?"

The man made a face as if to say, Oh yes? He smiled in the direction of his wife.

"Lots of trees are harvested just for making paper," John said as the woman came back to where he and her husband stood. Like her husband, she appeared to become riveted as she listened to John, who kept yakking away. "It's a good thing that more than forty-five percent of the paper now in use is recycled." The man's brow furrowed, and John said, "But, still, the majority of it comes from trees."

The woman said, "Is that so?"

John nodded. "And did you know that, just recently, we were cutting down the Amazon rainforest at a rate of almost thirty thousand square kilometers every single year?" The couple shook their head in unison, and John explained, "That's about three times the size of Puerto Rico."

58

ONE HUNDRED PLACES

When Nessa came out of the bathroom several moments later, she made a beeline toward John, whom the husband-wife pair was staring at wide-eyed. Nessa gave them a look of utter disapproval before telling them, "Excuse my friend." She took John by the hand and said, "Let's go."

John kept saying, "But we just got here Nessa. Let's stay." She ignored his supplications and dragged him back to the Oldsmobile. As John was driving away, he said to her, "You don't like them." He looked confused when she said,

"And what's there to like?"

John drove on I-72W for several hours; then he took I-35S and headed toward Kansas City. After following I-70W to Topeka, he got on US-50W, from where he merged onto E. Wyatt Earp Boulevard.

They visited Front Street and the Boot Hill Museum. Later the same day, John spotted some tourists who were riding on a stagecoach. He photographed them.

Twice, Nessa took her turn behind the wheel during the long return trip by way of I-70E. She was in a terribly bad mood as they passed Missouri, Illinois, and Indiana; because all John wanted to eat was his peanut-butter-and-jelly imitation-of-a-sandwich. Most times, she had to force him to eat proper food.

Sleeping was a problem too; for John had no qualms about spending the night at a rest stop. She was still sulking as she followed I-74E to I-75S.

As they entered Kentucky, John was saying, "I've already told you what it is I want to do here."

Nessa said, "You did."

They exchanged few words as they visited the Vent Haven's Ventriloquist Museum. Afterward, John got back behind the wheel and drove through Tennessee on I-65S. He merged onto I-20S in Alabama. Several hours later, he was following I-59S toward Louisiana. She was back at the wheel as the Oldsmobile drove over Lake Pontchartrain Causeway Bridge.

Nessa glared at John as he drove north on I-12. She said, "I don't understand."

"What don't you understand?" John said.

"I don't know. It's just that—look, I've turned it over and over in my head, and still can't make sense of any of it." She paused before saying, "Is there really a method to your madness?"

"No method, Nessa," John said. "And there's no plan either." After several moments, he said, "You know what I don't know?"

"No. I don't know what you don't know."

"I don't know why it is so hard for you to understand that I'm going to these places just so I can say, twenty years from now, 'I've been there. I've done that.'"

She said, "I get that, but I'm not referring only to the system—or lack thereof—you're using for getting us from point A to point B."

"No?" John said.

"Oh, no," said she. "I'm talking about you being all excited one moment about seeing a place, and then we get there, and all you do is drive through the effing place or past it. No stopping. No nothing." She was shaking her head from side to side. When John glanced at her and said nothing, she said, "Do   you   think   that's   normal?"

John exhaled through his mouth before speaking. "It's my trip, Nessa. You mustn't forget that."

"How   could   I?" she said. "You   won't   let   me." She adjusted herself on the seat and ended up with her back against the side of the car, facing him. "It's—like right now, for example. Why aren't we driving to Maine?" Even though it seemed that John wasn't paying attention by then, she added, "Have you changed your mind about following the book?"

ONE HUNDRED PLACES

John eyed her a full two seconds before saying, "I thought you didn't like that I was following the book. Didn't you say it wasn't efficient the way I was doing it?"

"I did," she said. That was so long ago, she thought. "But haven't you continued doing exactly that anyway? Since when do you listen to anyone? Since when do you listen to *me*?" She didn't understand why John was now grinning. "What kind of Aspie are you?!"

Not knowing at first why John, looking less aggrieved than peeved, had said, "Since you won't shut up," she was taken aback when the realization hit her that he'd been responding to the third in her barrage of questions. He said, "What do you know about Aspies anyway?"

She wanted to say something—anything to get him to shut up—but she didn't. And she didn't know why; neither did she know why she felt the strange sort of anger which began boiling inside of her, anger at the situation, anger at life, and at herself. She didn't hear him say, "Why didn't you stay the way you were?" John waited momentarily. "Hey!" He had raised his voice, which startled her. Bringing a trembling hand up to her mouth, she bit on her thumb nail. John said, "I think I liked you a lot better then."

"When?" she said.

"Before."

She thought aloud, "I can't believe this."

He said, "You're talking a bit too much now."

"Are you for real?" said she.

John said, "Made of flesh and blood. Aren't I?"

No, shit, thought Nessa.

He said, "I exist; so, yes, I'd say I'm for real."

"Uh-huh," she said.

"Doesn't that mean," he said, "that I get to make my own decisions?"

Nessa smirked as she said, "I guess so."

He said, "And I've decided to adjust my system a bit."

Whatever that means, she thought.

"We're going to Missouri now," he told her as the Oldsmobile merged onto the I-55N traffic.

She observed him awhile and began to purse her lips. Having decided at that moment to put a stop to their arguing, she wondered whether he'd be disappointed when she didn't complain. She liked this new John.

They arrived in Missouri and immediately went to visit the Museum of Westward Expansion. They also spent time watching groups of tourists enjoying the riverboat cruises. In the evening, they went back out; only so that John could take pictures of the Gateway Arch.

Had time slowed down? wondered a stressed-out Nessa as the Oldsmobile, with John at the wheel, started and stopped in the slow traffic they encountered along I-70W and I-29N. She began to relax a bit when the time came for her to drive; if only because the traffic was already clearing as she merged onto I-90W, which took them to I-15N.

In Montana, Nessa and other tourists climbed on board a 1930s 'Jammer' bus. They were going for a ride around Glacier National Park. John took several photographs of the bus as it departed; he did the same when it returned.

Nessa was at the wheel again around midday a few days later. She was driving down Las Vegas Boulevard.

They made it to the Hoover Dam, where Nessa convinced John to remain almost an hour so she could stretch her legs. Sort of morose at first, John seemed more relaxed after about ten minutes. He even allowed her to handle his disposable camera. She took a few pictures of him, the dam serving as the background.

When she got back on the road again, Nessa followed US-93N toward Las Vegas for several hours before turning onto NV-160W.

The Oldsmobile, with John at the wheel, was driving along Blue Diamond Road.

ONE HUNDRED PLACES

'Welcome to Pahrump. Heart of the New Old West,' said a sign on the side of the road.

"Pahrump?" Nessa said. "Such a weird name."

John said, "A weird name for a weird place. Pahrump is a census-designated place, a CDP."

"Never heard the term," said she.

At times, as they drove through the desolate town, stomach cramps caused Nessa to wince. She squirmed in her seat as both the intensity and the frequency of the cramps increased. And she would glance toward John as this was happening, but John seemed oblivious to everything but the road in front of him.

"A CDP," he said, "is what the Census Bureau calls any area that exists for the sole purpose of giving them data about a particular group of people."

She wasn't interested in any of it, but what could she do? Was she going to ask John to drop her off in the middle of nowhere? She pressed the back of her head against the seat's headrest and, as the Oldsmobile drove through Pahrump's desolate main street, she tried to ignore the stomach cramps.

"As such," continued John, "an area such as this doesn't even have legal boundaries."

She said, "That can't be possible."

"But it is," said he. "Pahrump exists in name only, and only as long as there are people living in it."

A bit confusing, she thought. "Is that right?" she said faking some interest.

John said, "Exactly."

But she wasn't convinced. "Okay. Let's do this. Let's say— if what you say is true—let's say, no one's living here right at this moment."

"Keep talking," John said.

"Does Pahrump exist right now, while we're driving through it?"

"Not according to what the definition of 'living' is," he said; "that is, not if by 'living' you mean 'residing.'"

Considering his point awhile, Nessa said, "You may be right." Then she wondered aloud, "Where do you learn these things?!"

He smiled and said, "I learned about this one right there." He pursed his lips and pointed toward the dashboard, at his book. "Books are our friends. You know?"

"I don't dispute that," she said.

They drove in silence several moments, after which John said, "I'm starving. Pass me the peanut butter, the jelly, and the bread." Nessa smiled to herself. After handing the items over, she spent some time observing him. "I'm also going to need two plastic spoons," he said.

"Sure thing." She handed those over, too, and continued watching him. He placed the two containers in between his legs and lay the bread on his thighs. God! she thought. Isn't he difficult! John stuck the spoons in either container, then ate a teaspoonful of peanut butter. He followed this with a piece of bread. A teaspoonful of jelly came next, then another piece of bread.

The ritual continued with John alternating between the peanut butter and the jelly until he'd eaten four slices of bread in this manner. All the while, a sense of bewilderment had seized Nessa. She just couldn't stop staring at him.

"Want one?" John said out of the blue.

"One what?" She felt embarrassed that he caught her staring. John said,

"A peanut butter and jelly sandwich."

"I don't think that what you're eating qualifies as a sandwich," she said. "Tell me. Why do you do that?"

"Do what?" Pointing at his lap, he drew circles over it with his finger. "This?"

She nodded. "Uh-huh."

"Because it tastes the same?" he said. "Because you don't have to waste energy and time putting it together? Must I really have a reason? Do you need one?"

ONE HUNDRED PLACES

She negated with her head while waving his offer aside with a hand. "I'm fine."

They continued heading east, toward South Rainbow Boulevard, on NV-160.

Except for the light from the Oldsmobile's headlamps, there was darkness all around the car as it drove in the open road. City lights appeared in the distance several moments later, and about twenty-five minutes after that, neon signs became visible as John and Nessa arrived in Enterprise, Nevada. The Oldsmobile entered a strip-mall parking lot.

John parked near the entrance to The Corner Bar. Nessa exited at once. She was wincing and holding on to her stomach as she body-slammed the car door shut with her hip.

"Where are you going?" John said, and she told him,

"I need to get away from this car for a while or I'm gonna go crazy." Her stomach cramps were getting worse. "Can you wait here?" As she spoke, she had been looking up and down the strip and considering the lay of the land. She settled on The Corner Bar. "Or you can go in there if you want." When John reached toward the back seat for his backpack, she said, "Ever go anywhere without that thing?"

"It never goes anywhere without me," said he. "What's inside?" He blinked every time he looked directly at the neon sign that adorned the façade of The Corner Bar.

"You're a big boy," she said. "Why not go find out for yourself?" She was still grabbing at her stomach. "Give me those keys please," she said.

"These are my keys," said John.

Pain shot up through her stomach. As she winced, she wondered whether John was even registering this. If he was, why didn't he comment on it? He commented on almost everything else. "Just give them to me," she said, and when John hesitated, she added, "I'll hold them for you." She took off as soon as he handed the keys over.

PEDRO VASQUEZ

Several seconds later, John and his backpack walked into a bar.

Fortunately for John, most of The Corner Bar patrons—and there weren't too many—were sitting by the stage, their eyes on their favorite 'exotic' dancer in the whole place.

His jaw dropped as he came in through the main entrance. He stopped dead in his tracks and began rubbing his eyes while trying to cover his ears at the same time. It was as if he could not stand the auditory and visual over-stimulation.

John seemed both mesmerized by the spectacle on the stage, and physiologically affected by the experience. He started backing away, but then two of the dancers appeared next to him and got in his space. They wore little to no clothes. John raised his hands and tried to shield his eyes from the lights. Which left his ears vulnerable to the loud music.

One of the dancers reached for John's back. She started rubbing it. As she did, the other dancer began stroking John's shoulder—just like Lily used to.

He appeared to relax.

The two women steered him deeper into the establishment. One of them snatched a couple of paper serviettes from the counter as they passed the main bar.

Nessa stood inside the entrance of The Corner Bar; just like John had about two hours earlier. Relieved that her stomach pain had subsided, she scanned the place for a few moments looking for John. She became worried when she didn't see him.

Several hostesses, including the two dancers who greeted him upon his arrival, were sitting across from John. They were in a darker corner of the bar and away from the strobe lights.

John had placed his backpack on the floor, in between his feet, and he looked more relaxed than usual as they talked—or as they listened; for he was doing most of the talking.

These ladies appeared genuinely interested in what he had to say.

"John," Nessa said when she spotted him. He didn't react. "John!" She had raised her voice several octaves, but John still appeared not to have heard her. Feeling more than a tad annoyed for reasons she was glad not to have to explain to anyone, Nessa squeezed in between two of the dancers.

"Hey, there," she said.

John noticed her this time. He grinned and, as if in a daze, said, "I... I..."

"Yes, you, you," said Nessa. "You ready?"

It looked like John was at a loss for words.

Nessa said to him, "Time to go, big boy," and offered her hand. He took it. She took the time to give each of the ladies around her a meaningful look before starting to drag him away.

Looking back just as they reached the exit, John waved. The dancers probably heard little of what he said to them. They smiled and waved enthusiastically nevertheless.

Nessa was leaning against the driver-side of the Oldsmobile, which was still parked in front of The Corner Bar. As she crossed to open the door moments later, John stood in front of her.

"What are you doing?" he said with boyish grin in his face. "You know I'm the designated driver tonight."

"You're under the influence," she was in the middle of telling him when she noticed something on the sides of John's face. "What's that?" she said, and John tilted his head back as she went to reach for it. He barely avoided her hands.

"I don't drink," he said. "This?" He took a rolled-up piece of paper out of each ear. "Earplugs."

"Those are pieces of paper you got there," she said.

"Acting as earplugs," said he.

Okay…, she thought. "You don't drink?" She wanted to change the subject.

John said, of the paper, "They attenuated the sound." He shook his head from side to side in answer to her question. "They did the job; so, they're earplugs."

"Whatever," Nessa said. "And what the heck were you doing in there all this time if not drinking?" He was about to answer, but she placed two fingers across his lips and said, "Shh. I don't wanna know."

John said, "Why ask the question if you're not interested in the answer?"

She was already walking around the front of the Oldsmobile. "It was a rhetorical question." On the other side of the car, she rested the palms of her hands on the roof. "That's why."

He said, "A what?"

"A rheto…," she'd begun to say, and then she caught John's drift. "Funny. Ha, ha. Here. Drive if you must." The keys slid across the roof of the Oldsmobile when she threw them at him.

John seemed rather elated a few moments later as he drove on South Las Vegas Boulevard. "Wow," he was saying. "Those ladies back there. They're really nice."

"Sure," Nessa said. "They *can* be very nice… How did you—?"

"I don't know. I was just talking."

"Right…," she said. "Aha. Don't tell me." Why should she believe him? she thought. "Probably cost you ten bucks each."

John said, "Thousand. Gave them ten thousand." He said it as if it were ten dollars he'd been talking about.

"Ten what?" She opened her eyes wide.

"A thousand, ten times," he said. "Didn't you see there were ten of them?"

ONE HUNDRED PLACES

Nessa shook her head from side to side, not in answer to the question but in disbelief. "You gave away ten thousand dollars just like that?" He nodded. "And where the heck did you get that kind of mon—?" She stopped suddenly. She could really use ten grand right now. As she caressed the inside of her right arm absentmindedly, John said,

"There's more where that came from."

"Oh, yes?" she said.

"Didn't I tell you I have money?"

She threw her head back and made a funny face. Why hadn't she taken him seriously the first time he mentioned the money? Because she'd thought he wasn't being serious; that's why. "So, you're rich?" she said affecting a male voice.

"No," said he. "But I have a few thousands."

It surprised her that the car was slowing down.

"Come see," John said.

Parked on the side of the road under the US Route 93/I-40 interchange, John was standing by the open trunk of the Oldsmobile, where Nessa came to join him.

John's large suitcase, with the clothes mostly back in it, was semi-closed—its zipper was broken. Having lifted a corner of the suitcase, John was sliding out from under it the brown briefcase Uncle Bonnie had given him.

There were dozens of loose one-hundred-dollar bills scattered on the floor of the trunk, under the suitcase.

Nessa got the surprise of her life when John opened the briefcase and she saw all the stacks of dollar bills—in twenties and fifties—he carried. "You must be crazy," she said stepping in front of him and reaching up to close the trunk after closing the briefcase. "Come on," she told him. She was already crossing to the front of the car when she looked back and saw that John had stayed put. "Let's go!"

The Oldsmobile was bathed in moonlight as it drove in the open road several hours later. Nessa was saying to John,

"I don't understand you. You've had that money back there all along, and every night we've been sleeping in the car or in some cheap motel?"

John was mum.

Maybe he's not listening? she thought. "You're so weird," she said. "You lead an easy, peanut-butter-bread-and-jelly-eating life; yet, at same time, you have no qualms about giving away thousands of dollars to complete strangers." She paused awhile. "I really don't get you." She rubbed her hands together for several moments as she glanced out her window. And then she said, "How much is in there anyway?"

He didn't answer.

"John."

"Huh?" he said finally.

"How much—?"

"Taking out ten thousand," he began to say, "one hundred fifty-six thousand six hundred fifty-one dollars and twenty-four cents."

He'd been listening... she thought, and she held her breath, sort of surprised, when there was a rattle.

Reaching up, John toggled the interior light on and glanced toward the ashtray. There was some loose change in there.

"And thirty cents," he said correcting his earlier tally.

"If that's the case," Nessa said, "could we please find a nice place to sleep—like, right now?

John said nothing, but a few moments later he took an exit ramp and headed toward Flagstaff, Arizona.

They were eating breakfast at a fast-food restaurant the following morning. "New Hampshire and New Jersey are a long way from here," Nessa was saying, her mouth half-full of food. "It'll take us forever to drive there, don't you think?"

"They're the next place in my book," John said.

"I know that," said she after washing down her food with a slurp of black coffee. "But I was thinking that maybe we

70

could jump to the next one." She had gone back to eating when John said,

"I want to go back to doing them alphabetically."

Nessa swallowed a mouthful of half-chewed food. At the same time, she stabbed her fork into the rest of her meal and sucked air into her lungs. "I understand what you want," she said. Needing to say much more—just to get it out of her chest—she was hesitant to instigate yet another argument, and just while they were eating. It was the only reason she waited as long as she did.

Unable to hold back any longer, Nessa said—within minutes of leaving the fast-food place—"We could still go to each—"

"What is it you want from me, Nessa?"

"Same thing as you," she said. Her heart was already beating faster, and she made herself pause and count to ten—too fast. "Look, John," she said. "We are on *this* side of the country." She had gestured with her hands to signify the Western United States. "Why couldn't we—why couldn't *you* adjust your plans a bit?"

John was blowing air through his mouth. He kept his eyes on the road as he grabbed his bottle of soda, which he was raising up to his lips when Nessa said,

"Just a tiny bit?"

"Okay, Nessa," he said after taking a big gulp from the bottle; and then he burped. "Sorry."

Excited at the resolution, Nessa reached for his arm. But he looked uncomfortable the moment she touched him. She withdrew her hand.

Nessa got behind the wheel a few hours after their little incident. She followed Interstate Highway 40 to New Mexico, where she took John spelunking at Carlsbad Caverns National Park. He seemed transfixed as he looked at the stalactites and stalagmites. The two of them visited the Gila Cliff Dwellings National Monument later the same day.

71

PEDRO VASQUEZ

John took US-180/US-191N to I-15N—there were signs for Salt Lake City on the road—then he followed I-84W to Boise, where they spent the night.

The next day, Nessa drove the rest of the way out of Idaho. In Portland, Oregon, they spent several hours walking about and browsing in Powell's City of Books, where Nessa sat down for a cup of coffee after putting in her bag a small package she had wrapped in funny-looking paper. John did share the table with her. However, he didn't say a word. Nessa found it ludicrous—and so annoying—that he would get upset because the bookstore did not have the issue of Popular Mechanics he'd gotten it in his head he had to have.

He didn't look any happier by the time they came out of the bookstore about thirty-five minutes later, and she said to him, "You know what? Perhaps it's time you realized the world doesn't have to revolve around you."

John said, "Never said it should."

"Stop behaving like a child then," she said.

"I'm not a child."

"My point exactly." Bursting with ire, Nessa threw her hands up in the air. She walked away under a cloudy sky, and John stayed behind sulking by the bookstore entrance. He hurried after her as she was about to disappear down the block.

John followed I-84E on their return trip from Oregon. In Boise, Idaho, he merged onto I-80E and continued toward Cheyenne. Noticing signs for Lincoln, Nebraska, Nessa thought she would let him drive a while longer. She took the wheel in Lincoln.

John was immersed in his book as Nessa followed I-29S to Kansas City. I-70E took her to St. Louis, Missouri. From there, she merged onto I-64E, which she followed to Richmond, Virginia.

ONE HUNDRED PLACES

John was spending time photographing the Wright Brothers Memorial Tower at Kill Devil Hill, in North Carolina. In the meantime, a serious-looking Nessa was strolling through the replica of a hangar that had been used by the Wright Brothers in the early 1900s. When they got back on the road, John took US-13N and US-113N to I-95N. The injuries on his face were barely noticeable by now.

John went by himself to visit Independence Hall, in Philadelphia, Pennsylvania. Nessa had decided to stay with the Oldsmobile. Sitting on top of the left front fender of the car, she smoked a cigarette as she waited for John.

Nessa came out of the bathroom. She had a towel wrapped around her wet hair.

"I thought about it enough," John said looking up from his book. He was sitting at the edge of the bed.

"Are you sure?" she said, and when he nodded, she added, "I want to hear you say it."

John seemed exasperated as he looked at her. "What do you want from me?" he asked.

"Not that much really," she said. "All I want is for you to say you agree that, yes, we will go to South Dakota, and after that, that you will either follow my lead or take my opinion into account."

He nodded again and scowled at her.

Was he trying to upset her? she thought. He had succeeded; for she had gone from merely peeved to infuriated in a millisecond. Miraculously, however, she managed to bite her tongue. Her heavy, arrhythmical breathing was the only overt measure of the state she was in.

"Okay, okay," he said grinning.

"I want to hear the words," she said.

"I agree, Nessa." He paused a few moments. "But you shouldn't push me." He had turned serious. "I don't like being pushed around."

"Okay," she said glaring at him. She found his tone rather menacing. It was why she felt compelled to say afterward, "Just so you know. That's not what I was doing." Did she see him relax some after she'd faked a smile?

They were near Pittsburgh, Pennsylvania; going west on Interstate 76. Nessa was feeling nervous. She had an inkling she probably looked the part too. Fidgety, when she wasn't interlacing her fingers back and forth, she was running the palm of one hand slowly against the other. She glanced in John's direction whenever she thought he wasn't looking. There was a weird sensation in the pit of the stomach as she began to see him in a different light. It was as if the thoughts brewing in her mind were causing infant butterflies to flap their wings. She nibbled on her thumb, which she was pressing sideways against her teeth.

The Oldsmobile was parked at a rest area. John lay stretched out on the driver seat as far as the space would allow. It was around 1:00 a.m.

Was he asleep? Nessa wondered as she lay on the back seat, her feet almost touching John's head. Watching him, she realized she had no idea why he hadn't just kept driving until they found a motel. Oh, well.

She was careful not to make noise when, about an hour later, she was pushing the door open. Holding on to the car's frame, she slid her feet out from under John's reclined seat and pulled herself out of the car. She walked around the front to the driver-side and stuck a hand in through the window. Her hand avoided John's leg as it traveled toward the trunk-release.

There was a muted pop two seconds later when the trunk opened. John's eyes opened. Strands of Nessa's long hair were touching his legs. He remained still as the arm snaked back out of the car.

When she looked at him, his eyes were closed.

ONE HUNDRED PLACES

John's briefcase sat open in the semi-darkness of the trunk. Nessa collected the bills that were scattered about it and crammed them inside. After closing it, she used both hands to lift the briefcase out of the trunk. She deposited it outside on the ground and caught herself as she went to slam the trunk lid shut. Frozen momentarily, she then brought it down slowly and stopped short of closing it. She was beginning to back away from the car when John's eyes became visible through the rear windshield. They were staring back via the interior rear-view mirror.

The first light of day hit the road sign: Welcome to Fox Run (pop. 3,544). Nessa hurried past it seconds later, John's briefcase swinging in her hand. Her silhouette was disappearing in the distance by the time the Oldsmobile appeared. The car was inching along behind her.

Nessa laid the briefcase on the floor of the local bus and planted her feet on top of it. Reclining on her seat, she smiled a sad smile. It had not given her any pleasure stealing from John. On the contrary, she already felt burdened by a heavy sense of guilt. Dread at continuing in her current life, however, loomed larger still than all her guilt. She didn't want to remain an addict. She didn't want to die a junkie. She convinced herself that her bad deed had been for a good cause. Now she had enough cash to put herself through a treatment program. It was the only way of kicking her habit, she thought as her eyes closed.

It was still early in the morning, and there was not another soul around. A bleary-looking Nessa came out of the interstate bus terminal. She put her ticket away as she followed the sidewalk along the front of the terminal and went to sit on a bench about forty-five feet from the entrance. Standing the briefcase on her lap, she rested her hands and chin on it as she waited. Another ten minutes, and she would be on her way.

John had kept well behind the local bus, which passed several small towns as it was covering its route. He noticed Nessa through the windshield when he neared the interstate bus terminal.

She saw the Oldsmobile drive by and didn't flinch. The car disappeared around a bend on the street; less than two minutes later, it was driving back in the opposite direction.

Having parked across from the bus terminal, John rubbed his eyes as he crossed the street. And he didn't say a word, but as soon as he sat down next to her, Nessa got to her feet and placed the briefcase on his lap.

John was driving. He reached for his book and laid it against the steering wheel. As he thumbed through the pages, Nessa said,

"Where to next?" John didn't answer. "We shouldn't be carrying all this money around. You know?" He still didn't acknowledge her and just kept dividing his attention between the road and the book. "I—I was going to find a safe place for it." A long minute passed. John didn't say a word. "Aren't you gonna say anything? Tell me off or something?" It was as if she weren't there next to him. She sighed.

John didn't even glance in her direction when he finally said, "My Ma said that it's better to say nothing when one has nothing good to say."

"And John?" said she.

He rubbed his eyes. "What?" He looked tired.

Nessa said, "What does John think?"

He said, "You want to be reprimanded, Nessa?"

"Don't I deserve it?"

He both looked and sounded composed when he told her, "Nessa, please, don't do that again"; and he showed zero emotion when she said,

ONE HUNDRED PLACES

"Now. How hard was that?"

It was mid-afternoon several weeks later, and John was driving on the open road. Nessa was tapping on her thighs to the music playing on the car radio. About twenty minutes later, John took an exit ramp and headed toward Mount Rushmore National Park, South Dakota.

The Oldsmobile was parked near the entrance to Mount Rushmore, and Nessa was standing outside the driver-side door. John hurried out of the car a minute later. Looking more cheerful than his usual self, he said,

"Let's go explore!"

"*Vamos!*" said Nessa as she sniffed the fresh air. She was so happy for him.

Having locked on to her use of Spanish, John could be heard beginning a lecture on the proper way to conjugate the verb '*Ir*' (to go) as they headed through the trees into the park.

Several moments later, after they had explored a good portion of the park grounds, John stopped for a while and looked at the presidential busts. He kept looking at the busts when he came to sit next to her on the grass. And all the while, she had been watching him.

John stood up after about ten minutes and began pacing in front of her. "Did you know?" he said. "Many people opposed the creation of this monument because the government seized the land from the Lakota tribe to build it."

She yawned; the subject did not interest her. "Why stop here?" she said awhile later. "Why is it that this place is even important?" John's brow furrowed, and she thought, He probably thinks I'm uncultured. John opened his eyes wide, as if he were surprised at her remark, and shook his head ever so slowly. Nessa said, "What. They're all dead. Aren't they?" Casting his eyes down, John seemed distant several moments, and she thought, Here he goes again.

White contrails had materialized against a blue sky. The outline of an airplane was discernible ahead of them.

In the chapel during Lily's funeral service, the priest was about to begin his sermon. John was sitting in the front row, his eyes fixed upon his mother's casket. Helen, who along with Ariadne and Iris was sitting behind John, said, "What has he done with his life?"

John was sitting on the sofa in Lily's living room. It was just after the burial. Sitting across from him on an identical sofa, Samantha was saying, "Lily's in a better place now, John."

He appeared not to have heard her; his attention was set on the pictures that hung on the wall, behind her. In In one of the photos, Lily was cradling him as a baby.

The muffled conversation of Helen, Ariadne, and Iris drifted in from the kitchen. "I wonder what he'll do now," Helen said.

"Probably not much," said Ariadne. "History tends to repeat itself."

Iris said, "He'll probably just sit in this house 'til he dies, I suppose—just like poor Lily."

John swallowed. His gaze drifted downward.

John lifted his gaze, and Mount Rushmore appeared in all its glory. He stared at it.

But this was no blank stare: His eyes were darting from one side to the other in their sockets as if his mind were racing. He blinked several times.

"They're important, these men," he said.

"Why are they important, John?" Nessa said.

Lowering his head, Johns said, "I don't know." He looked at her. "All of them were presidents. I guess that makes them…" He sighed. "I haven't done anything with my life." It looked as if he were about to retreat into his mind once again.

She said. "You *are* important too. We all are." She managed to subdue the urge to burst out laughing. Did she believe a word of what she had just said? She tried to smile, show him some humanity. She couldn't.

"Look at it this way, John" she said. "At least you're not stuck in Kansas anymore, *Doroteo*." She was surprised when he didn't get the reference.

John sat back down at her side, "Does that count for anything?"

"It has to count for something," she said. She started stroking his back. "If you asked me, I'd say you don't need to go to the moon or be president to be important." She stopped talking awhile, after which she said, "It's getting dark; we should go."

They headed west on Interstate 70 when they left Mount Rushmore. She was at the wheel.

The following day, the Oldsmobile was stopped on the side of the road in the Mojave Desert, Utah.

Nessa leaned sideways against the hood of the car as she smoked a cigarette. She peered into the car through the windshield. John was sitting in the passenger seat looking upset as he handled his disposable camera. The device had run out of film. "We can get another one," she said.

"Why don't we go get it now?" said John as he came to stand in front of her.

She threw what was left of her cigarette on the ground and stepped on it. She was about to get in the car when John said, "Are you going to leave that there?" He was pointing at the cigarette butt. She gave him the finger, and he said, "An ugly gesture. You must be ugly inside."

Her mouth closed, Nessa was rubbing her tongue over her upper teeth—her teeth needed brushing—when John asked her, "Are you ugly inside, Nessa?" She just got in the car and slammed the door shut as he was bending down to pick up her litter.

Albert stood behind the counter of a gas station quick-stop on US-191 North. Sixty, short, and balding, he was watching his two new customers, John and Nessa. They were making their way through the three aisles of the store.

Willie was in his mid-twenties. He was attractive in a run-down sort of way, but the strategically placed tattoos covering his forearms couldn't disguise the needle marks. As he stocked the store shelves, he too turned to look at the new arrivals; especially at Nessa, whose demeanor helped him recognize her as a fellow druggie.

"You're the one with the money," Nessa was saying to John. When she handed him two disposable cameras, he immediately crossed toward the front of the store.

"They don't make them like they used to. Do they?" she heard Albert say to John as the latter placed the cameras on the counter, near the register. Arriving at the back aisle, she feigned interest in some of the items displayed in front of her. She even grabbed a small bag of cookies, which she examined perfunctorily before replacing it on the shelf. She glanced toward the counter, then at Willie; he was looking at her too. She once again glanced toward the front of the store. Albert had apparently engaged John in conversation.

Willie stopped what he was doing and moved in on her. They spoke quietly some brief moments—Nessa was doing most of the talking.

Meanwhile at the front of the store, John was scanning the myriad products set strategically about the counter. And he was saying, "I think the one-hundred-and-twenty-millimeter film was much better." He looked toward the back aisles, where Willie and Nessa were disappearing around a corner.

"Myself," said Albert, "I find the nine-millimeter superior."

ONE HUNDRED PLACES

Willie was kissing Nessa, but she was not responding. He slid his hands over her blouse and started fondling her breasts.

After she'd let him do this for about five seconds, Nessa grabbed those hands and eased her trunk away from Willie's. He continued to kiss her. What are you doing? she thought.

Her head pivoted back on her neck, ending the kiss, and she extended her right arm and slowly rolled up her sleeves. There were no tattoos to cover her bruises and purple marks—the result of countless injections of heroin.

It was about twenty minutes later. Drug paraphernalia lay scattered about Nessa and Willie. Both of them looked high as they sat on the floor. The drug, however, appeared to have a greater effect on Willie. His head wobbled toward her as he attempted another kiss, which he didn't get the chance to deliver because she already was getting to her feet. She lowered her shirtsleeve after twice bending and extending her arm.

John had been pacing by the counter, and Nessa saw him glance toward the rear of the store at the exact moment that she was sneaking back in from behind the wall. She scurried toward the aisle where the cameras were.

Albert rang up John's purchase: two disposable cameras, a pack of Post-it notes, and some gum. There was a chemically induced air of nonchalance about Nessa as she approached the counter two minutes later. She handed John two more disposable cameras.

"What are you doing?" he said glaring at her.

"I figure we'll need a couple more."

He snatched the cameras from her hands and threw them on the counter. Albert looked up at him.

When the store manager looked at her, Nessa wondered whether he could discern the state she was in. She noticed the disapproval in his face, and the hint of pity which followed.

She was quiet as the Oldsmobile was merging onto I-80 East and leaving the gas station in the past. Feeling like a kid who's done something naughty and hopes no one finds out, she looked straight ahead and tried not to blink, lest John notice her.

"You went with him to do drugs," John said after they had been on the road several minutes.

"Well," she said, "at least I didn't *friend* him." Her words seemed to go right over John's head.

"You don't want to stop," he said, and this surprised her. She had never expected him to speak this way. Who the heck did he think he was?

"That's my business," she said. Don't judge."

"I don't judge," said he. "I state facts. And from what I gather, it seems you're not going to stop."

She looked out the window and mumbled, almost to herself, "Like I said, my business. Worry about your own damn self, or walk a mile in my shoes, *then* talk."

John was looking at her through squinting eyes. Scratching his head, he put his attention back on the road.

A starry sky canopied US Route 287 as they headed north on the open road. Nessa had been quiet a long while; now she felt like making conversation. "How many stars are there?" she said.

"Depends," said John. "With the naked ey—"

"You know?" she said. "You would get much more enjoyment out of life if you stopped analyzing everything all the time."

He said, "Ha! Enjoy life. But if life itself was basically an accident. Nothing but the random interaction of atoms."

She felt like smacking him—softly, on his lips.

"Didn't you get the memo?" he said. "Life will happen regardless of whether you enjoy it or not."

"See?" Nessa said. "That's what I'm talking about. Don't you *feel* anything?" She really wanted to sound annoyed, but she knew her demeanor said something much different.

"I loved Ma," he said.

"Exactly," said she. "You loved her. Isn't there anyone else you love?"

He said, "Nobody else is my mother—Oh, yes. I love science and mathem—"

"I'm talking about people, John." Her annoyance came across when she added, "You, dummy."

"I don't know," John said. "And, Nessa—" He, too, sounded annoyed now—"please don't call me a dummy. Okay? Ma didn't like it when people said I was dumb; I don't think I like it either." Oh shit, she thought.

"John. I'm sorry. I didn't mean—"

"Dumb is an ugly word," he said. "And you're not that ugly." He grinned, and she couldn't help smiling at his unexpected compliment.

She said, "I swear I didn't mean anything by it," and she averted her eyes when he looked at her.

Nessa was driving. Sun rays bent over the hood of the Oldsmobile as she merged onto I-90E. She squinted as they hit her eyes.

Several hours later, she was following John around at Devils Tower National Monument. He pointed at the rock formations and was about to speak.

She cut him off. "Did you know that this type of mountain is called laccolith?" John look surprised. "It is basically viscous magma injected in between two sedimentary rocks." She was smirking as she continued. "What you're looking at now is not even the real thing."

John said, "No?"

"No. Erosion has completely damaged—" Bummer, she thought. She scratched her head. "Forgot the rest."

John stood in front of her, his mouth agape.

She said, "How did I do it?" and she snickered when he didn't answer. "See?"

He looked rather annoyed.

Later the same day, as Nessa drove on US-14 South, she said, "After the next stop, we hit Seattle. Then, we'll basically be done with this side of the world. You see?"

"I see," said John. "See what?"

Whatever, she thought, and flapped a hand at him dismissively. She merged onto I-90N several hours later.

As they strolled about Sacagawea's birthplace, in Idaho, she took the lead.

The Oldsmobile sped down a long stretch of road in the outskirts of a desert town. Liner mats covered either side of this road—light green ones on one side, and dark green one on the other.

"What are those?" Nessa said.

"They're phosphorous and nitrogen mats."

"Never seen any such thing before. What the heck are they for?" Before John could even begin to answer, she added, "Looks like a waste of material, whatever it is. Why do this out here in the middle of nowhere?" She kept looking from one side to the other of the road, intrigued, as John said,

"The light-green ones are full of nitrogen. They're used so that the grass doesn't have to pull as much water from the soil. The darker ones are enriched with phosphorous, so it needs less fertilizer to grow."

"Why use two different kinds?"

"I don't know, Nessa. Why do you use drugs?" He hadn't skipped a beat.

"God!" She was bursting with anger. "Shit doesn't concern you! Why don't you stop meddling in my business?" As John scratched his chin, she said, as if to herself, "You're such an asshole sometimes."

ONE HUNDRED PLACES

John said, "I'm no asshole." Exhaling through her mouth didn't help her calm down. She produced a cigarette, which she was about to light when John said,

"You can't smoke in the car." Nessa glowered at him. "Did you forget Ma's rule?" She affected a mockingly innocent tone when she said,

"Is it still in effect?"

John said, "It's her car."

"She's dead, John. I'd advise you to remember that sometime." John's lips quivered, and his nostrils palpitated after he gulped. I'm doing him a favor, Nessa thought as he sighed. "This is your car now. You're not *borrowing* it from her or anything like that anymore." She lit her cigarette, took a long drag, and blew the smoke toward his face. "I'm pretty sure she won't mind."

The tiny bit of guilt she felt at how awfully sad John looked after her reference to Lily, would drive her to find a way to atone.

John was pushing a shopping cart down the aisle of a supermarket. Nessa picked food items from the shelves and threw them in the cart. She stopped to watch him. "What's up?" she said.

John's look was one of dumbfoundedness as he stood in the middle of the aisle, looking left and right, his hands palm-up in front of his chest. "Why are there so many things here?"

"It's a supermarket, John." She wondered whether it was his first time inside one of these mega stores.

"But why do they have so many different names on the same kind of products?" he said as they continued down the aisle.

"So that people have choices, I guess." She turned at the end of the aisle. "At different prices," she said. "You know?" She was smitten when she arrived at the next aisle and saw what was on display.

Alcoholic beverages.

She looked at John. From that point on, all kinds of ideas started brewing in her mind. Poor John: he was clueless, and she knew it. She said, "It's supposed to tell them which of them is the better product—sort of."

"Just because it is more expensive?"

She wasn't too convinced about this one point. "I don't know, John."

"And why are the cheaper ones on the lower shelves? Isn't it harder for people to see them?" Nessa did not try to conceal the twinkle of mischief that sparkled in her eyes as she stooped to grab a bottle Absolut Vodka and one of Triple Sec. Down the aisle, she picked up cranberry and lime juice. John said, "What if they have back or knee problems and can't bend down?"

"Then," she said, "they get stuck with the better product." She looked him in the eyes. "They get lucky." She had been grinning from ear to ear as she said this last bit; still, John appeared not to have caught the insinuation.

The briefcase with John's money stood next to the bed, at the edge of which John sat paging through his book.

After she was finished lining up cooking ingredients on the kitchenette counter, Nessa mixed herself a batch of cosmopolitan. She poured herself a drink and, in the hour that followed, managed to put dinner together while drinking and dancing about the little motel room John had chosen for them to spend the night in.

They had already eaten. Cocktail spilled on the cheap tablecloth as Nessa refilled her glass. She looked at John, and even though she could've just as easily extended a hand and handed it to him, she left her chair and crossed to the other end of the table, where John was sitting. She offered him the same medium-sized tumbler she'd been drinking from.

"No," he said.

ONE HUNDRED PLACES

She was shaking her head from side to side as she came back to her chair. Staring at him, she raised the glass to her lips. She didn't swallow the mouthful of cocktail right away; instead, she started swishing it in her mouth, a sommelier out on a wine-tasting tour. She gulped, and again extended her glass toward John.

He negated with his head.

She insisted, and John again refused. After drinking some more, she emptied what was left of the cosmopolitan into the tumbler. She looked at him as she used her finger to give the contents of the glass a couple of swirls, then she licked the finger.

John stood up and went into the bathroom. When he came back into the room, he went straight to bed.

He must be tired, Nessa was thinking as she walked past the bed moments later. As usual whenever she wasn't by herself, she opened the bathroom-sink tap before sitting down on the toilet.

The next day, the Oldsmobile followed US-93N and I-90W to Seattle, Washington.

A salmon wiggled its tail as it flew sideways over a countertop. A second later, a fisherman caught it.

John was looking everywhere, fascinated, as this was happening. Nessa, bored out of her mind, was leaning sideways against a wall, supervising him. She refused to actually participate in the hustle and bustle of Seattle's Pike Place Market.

From the Space Needle observation deck a few hours later, John was taking pictures of the downtown Seattle skyline.

Nessa pointed toward Mt. Rainier and Lake Union as she spoke with a couple of tourists. The three of them were standing opposite John at the other end of the platform.

It was late afternoon. Nessa was driving. Sitting quietly at her side, John was examining his book, of which about two-thirds of the pages were marked with Post-it notes already. Glad that they again would be spending the night at a motel—instead of in the car—Nessa tapped her fingers on the steering wheel as she took an exit ramp and started to follow a local road.

Nessa was drinking and dancing about the room—just as before—as she made dinner. She smiled to herself each time she eyed John, who never lost sight of his briefcase. Was it because he held a grudge? Some people didn't know how to forgive.

They finished eating. Nessa rose from her chair and went to set her half-full tumbler of cosmopolitan in front of John before coming back to her chair. In a variation of the *Añjali Mudra* gesture typical of some Asian countries, she pressed her hands together in front of her chest and 'begged.' He wouldn't drink. She insisted and insisted until, finally, he obliged and picked up the glass.

But he set it back down almost immediately, surprising her. "I want a clean glass," he said.

"What did you just say?"

John said, "A new one, I mean."

He's drunk, Nessa was thinking less than forty minutes later. She'd been watching him. He'd taken various sips from his drink just within the last ten minutes. She was inebriated herself. Drawing on her alcohol-induced 'courage,' she went to sit by him. John seemed relaxed—in an awkward sort of way, or as best as he was capable of relaxing. He's drunk, she repeated in her mind, the recurring thought spurring her on. She began stroking his arm.

Shit, she thought soon afterward. Despite being only too eager to put the moves on him once and for all, she forced herself to slow down. She did not want to scare him. You're going all tender now? she wondered as she went back to just watching him.

ONE HUNDRED PLACES

When she offered John her hand a short while later and he took it, her thoughts took her back to the night when she had to drag him out of the strip club. Wasn't it funny how she'd gotten all worked-up at seeing him surrounded by all those women? What the heck had all that been about?

Letting himself be led to the bed, John fell flat on his face upon reaching it.

"No, no, no," she said. "Come here, you."

His eyes were closed, and this made her wonder whether he was asleep already. Turning him on his back, she lay on top of him and started kissing him. John seemed to respond at first. He opened his eyes and pressed his hands on her chest. Thinking he was trying to push her off him, she took his head in her hands and kept kissing him. But then she noticed that he actually looked sick and was trying to sit up.

"What is—?" she began to say, and she barely had time to move her face out of the way before the stream of vomit came at her. "What the f...?" It landed on her shoulder. *Recórcholis!* (Good heavens!) she thought. She grabbed him by the arms—"Come"—and tried to pull him off the bed. She couldn't.

He was shaking his head. "I'll sleep on the floor."

"No," she said.

He said, "It's okay."

John lathered his hair with shampoo in the shower the next morning.

Having put on clean clothes, he was drying his head with a towel when he returned to the room.

"Here you go." Nessa offered him a glass of water and two slices of bread.

"Bread?" he said.

"No," she said. "Cake."

He turned his head to the sides slightly, as if to say, Okay...

"Take it," she said. "It'll absorb the booze."

John took the offering. "Is this a cure for how I feel?" he said after he'd taken a bite out of one of the slices of bread.

"Should make you feel a lot better." She watched him eat in silence awhile.

"Sorry I regurgitated on you," John said. "I read that the Romans used to do it all the time after their huge me—" He turned his face as she went to kiss him.

"Shh," she said, and when she tried again, he pulled away. You're not going to escape, she thought. She embraced him and kept trying to kiss him.

John said, "Why kiss?" He kept turning his head from one side to the other and avoiding her mouth. "I don't feel anything when you kiss me."

"What?" she thought aloud, confused.

He said, "Why smack your face against another and exchange saliva? It can't be healthy. Mouths have germs, you know?" She rolled her eyes when he said, "I threw up earlier." Pressing a finger against his lips, she told him,

"Shh. Shut up. The mouthwash killed all those germs." She went for it once again.

"But the smell remains," he said. "And I've said no." He had raised his voice.

She released her grip on him and moved away, deflated. A few moments later, she went to bed. John joined her in bed minutes later, and while he fell asleep almost immediately, she spent quite a long time tossing and turning at his side. She was hot, and it had nothing to do with the weather.

John looked uncomfortable as he and Nessa strolled down Hollywood's Walk of Fame a few weeks later. It occurred to Nessa that perhaps it was because of the hordes of people coming and going all around him. She swore she felt him relax a bit whenever she stroked his shoulders or ran the tips of her fingernails along the length of his back.

ONE HUNDRED PLACES

It was just before dusk now, and they were standing in front of the Kodak Theatre. John seemed somewhat more at ease; maybe because there were not too many other people around. As they sauntered down the street and Nessa interlaced her fingers with his, he pulled his hand away. She kept trying, and he kept disentangling his fingers from hers. Every time, he would then take her hand in his—but as a parent would a kid's. This went on for quite a while; until she got tired of the game and let go.

John was lying in bed in another cheap motel several days later, his face one of confusion and fear. Empty beer bottles sat on the table next to his briefcase. Reclining on a couch across from the bed, Nessa had been watching him for several moments. She left the couch and came to sit next to him at the edge of the bed.

"You don't have a fever," she told him after feeling his forehead. "It's just a hangover." She left the bed, picked up her bag, and went into the bathroom. She handed John two Tylenols and a cup of water when she returned. "Why haven't you told me anything about yourself, about your family?" She had wanted to ask this question long ago but was afraid of what John's reaction would be. "I don't even know where you come from."

John blinked a few times before opening his eyes wide. He said matter-of-factly, "Because talking about my family means talking about my father. I don't like talking about him."

"Why?" she said.

John said, "I don't think I like being hungover either."

"No one does." She waited, and when he didn't say more, she said, "It's okay. You don't have to talk if you don't feel like it." She lay herself down next to him and allowed three seconds to tick by. "You know," she said, "you could—isn't there anything at all you can share with me?" He almost smiled. She said, "Don't you see? We've been together all this

91

time… It isn't normal that we don't know more of each other."

"My Ma," John said just after his face had registered a hint of annoyance. "She was nice to me. Taught me everything I know."

"Like what?" She rested her chin in her cupped hands.

He said, "She taught me to read, to do math—"

"You didn't go to school—?" She'd been about to add 'like normal kids,' but stopped this line of reasoning when she realized what she would've been implying. Afraid that he was going to interject, she was relieved when he didn't. "I'm sorry," she said. "So, you didn't do as the other kids in your neighborhood?"

"Like the *normal* kids?" John said, his fingers setting the third word in quotes and adding to the emphasis he had imparted to it.

She thought, *You* can put it like that.

"There weren't a lot of kids around where I grew up," he said. "No schools nearby either." He paused. "Yes, I was home-schooled, and Ma was my—"

"She was your teacher." John nodded. "I see," she said, her voice low, as if she were talking to herself. She felt a tad sad when he said,

"She was my everything."

She said, "That's what it sounds like."

"She helped me with homework too."

Of course, Nessa thought. "She didn't hold a regular job?"

He said, "She worked at the library."

"That's a regular job," said Nessa.

"Growing up, I was always with her at the library," he said, "if I wasn't at work. Read all the time. Could read all day given the chance!"

Nessa smiled; for she had just found the answer to another of the questions she'd been asking herself about him. "No wonder you know so much about so many subjects."

"I only know that I know nothing," John said.

ONE HUNDRED PLACES

She said, "You do know a lot—but do you ever use your own words, though: that is the question."

"Not according to Socrates," he said regarding her first point. "And yes, I do use my own words most times." He paused as if for effect. "However, he's been dead awhile—Socrates. So, I don't think he'd mind."

"Who?" She giggled. She knew whom John was referring to.

He said, "I'm not as dumb as I look, Nessa."

"I know," she said. "And believe it or not, as pleasing as I am to the eyes, it's quite possible I'm even more intelligent than beautiful." Having started laughing, she put on a mock-angry face when he said,

"Which doesn't mean you're any wiser."

"Hmm," she said. "Well-read and with money. The perfect man."

"Almost," John said. "I don't like to kiss and," he became serious "according to you, I can be a real prick sometimes."

She grinned. "Sorry, my friend," she said. "Not everyone can be completely perfect like me." Resting her head on her folded arms, she soon fell asleep.

The midday sun scorched the landscape all around as John's Oldsmobile sped down the highway under the Arizonian skies. Radio music was playing. Nessa glanced at John, who was sound asleep on the reclined passenger seat, the wrappings of fast food at his feet.

The sound of a shower running drifted into the motel room as Nessa sat in bed watching TV. From time to time, she would glance at John's briefcase. It was leaning against the couch on John's side of the bed.

There was leftover pizza and an empty bottle of wine on the table later that night as, on the bed, Nessa straddled John, who was lying face up on the bed. It seemed sort of funny to her that he was having difficulties putting the simplest of

93

sentences together. And it wasn't that John was drunk as he had been before. His 'problem' was that she was kissing and nibbling at his ears and neck. She paused long enough for him to say,

"I was born John S. Peter, in Ulysses, Kansas. My mother told me that I hadn't even begun to walk when my father left us." He was looking mortified as Nessa kept taking liberties with him.

She not only looked the part, but she also felt aroused. "Mmm. Yeah," she whispered in John's ears—as if it were *him* pecking at her ears and neck, and not the other way around. "And what does the S stand for? Tell me more." John said nothing, but recognition did wash over his face. "I bet it stands for sexy," she said.

"My middle name was not spelled out on my birth certificate." He turned thoughtful. "Ma never told me, and I never asked." He paused. "It was probably what they call a defense mechanism on her part."

"How so?" She knew the term, but she had no clue how it applied to 'his Ma.'

"Maybe she didn't want to repeat a certain name?" John said. "Who knows."

"And you were never curious?" she said.

"Not in the least," said he.

A defense mechanism on *your* part, she thought. "It has to be sexy. Very sexy."

Giving her an amused grin, he said, "Could be *simpático* too.'

"Ha!" she said. "I doubt that very much."

Nessa glided toward the bathroom several moments later. John stayed in bed, the sheets pulled up to his chin and an Oh-My-God expression etched on his face. He had just had his first experience with sex with another person.

PART III

Nessa headed east on Interstate 40 the following day.

In the afternoon, she was driving on a nondescript road on the outskirts of a city in New Mexico. The city was like Los Angeles in that you could see the cityscape as the Oldsmobile went over a hill.

"Hey. Wake up," she said. John was curled up asleep in the passenger seat. He opened his eyes for an instant, rolled over, mumbled something she could not understand, and went back to sleep. "Where the heck are we dude?" He didn't respond, she raised her voice. "Wake up!" She smirked when her yelling startled him. Semi-awake now, John rubbed his eyes as he glanced at their surroundings before looking at her. "Where are we?" she said. Squinting in the sunlight, he looked at the Post-it notes she had affixed to the steering wheel days before.

"Good morning, Nessa," he said. "How are you today? Did you sleep well?"

IBM's Watson could show more feelings than that, she thought. "Please, don't try so hard," she said. "I beg you."

"Okay," he said. He seemed confused. "How come you're driving?" She gave him a look before putting her attention back on the road and smiled to herself.

"How funny," she said. "Thought I was much more memorable than that." John's brow furrowed. He looked even more confused when she told him, "We left morning way back in Arizona." She slid her bottom lip up against the top one and let air escape through her mouth. As she did, strands of hair waved over her brow. "You really don't remember. Do you?"

He said, "Is it supposed to make one so tired?" He observed their surroundings once again. "Where are we?"

"I dunno. LA, I think?" she said. And then she noticed he was frowning. "It looks like it." In answer to his first question, she said, "At the rhythm you do it, yes, one could get tired."

"How long have we been——?" John had started to say before he stopped in his tracks. "Did you say LA?!" It seemed his brain had connected the dots. "We are not in the right place, Nessa. We should be heading——"

"I said it *looked* like LA; not that it was." She was digging for something in between her thighs as she spoke. She pulled out a piece of paper. "Had you given me something other than cryptic codes…," she said, and the paper made a crunching noise as she made it into a ball, "…maybe we would've been heading in the right direction." She flung the ball of paper at him and he caught as it flew in front of him. Unfolding it, he ironed out the wrinkles with his hands.

"These directions are fine," he said looking at his scribblings.

"Beg to differ," said she. "I need to stop."

"We don't need to stop," John said after looking at the fuel gauge. He then proceeded to read from the piece of paper in his hand. "Head east by northeast for one point thirty-six miles. Turn——"

"My point exactly," Nessa said. "Anyway, I'm gonna pee in my pants if I stay in this car a minute longer." She was taking an exit ramp already, and was surprised when there was no retort from John. "Hey!"

He'd fallen asleep once again.

ONE HUNDRED PLACES

The muffled sound of yelling awakened John about twenty-five minutes later. The Oldsmobile was parked at a gas station.

Nessa stood several yards away from the car. Stoned, she was screaming at the top of her lungs at the attendant, who had a cell phone to his ears. He spoke a few words into it before ending the call and putting the device in his pocket, then he just stood there eyeballing Nessa.

She paced in front of the man and cursed him in Spanish each time she changed direction. With every step, she slipped in and out of the drug-induced fog she was navigating. It was during these fleeting moments of lucidity that she would glance toward the Oldsmobile. The attendant kept checking his watch. From time to time, he would glance toward the road, beyond which a gang appeared about ten minutes later.

John seemed hesitant as he left the safety of the Oldsmobile and walked toward 'the situation.'

As her row with the gas station attendant continued, Nessa noticed John. Her demeanor changed. It became more subdued the closer John got to her.

The attendant was saying, "Don't you worry, *tu hora ya llegó* (your time has come). The gang's presence appeared to have emboldened him.

"What's going on?" John said. He was looking back and forth between Nessa and the attendant. "Can I help?"

"Who the heck are you?" the attendant said turning to look at him. "You better—"

"This assho—" Nessa had begun saying to John. Her words became slurred; she could not even understand herself. John said to the attendant,

"She's my friend."

Nessa said, "I just wanted—"

"You can fuck right off," the attendant said to John, but almost immediately, he changed his tune to, "Unless you wanna pay for the shit she broke." A gang of Black,

97

Caucasian, and Hispanic boys and girls (in their late teens and early twenties) surrounded John and Nessa.

Their leader came within striking distance of the former. Gesturing with her head at the attendant: 'What's up?' she said to him, "Hey, homie. This the *pendeja* (idiot, moron)?"

He nodded. "*Sí*. She wanted smack. As if..."

"I'm sorry," Nessa said to John. Tears already welled in her eyes. The gang leader said to the attendant,

"...because you sure look like a drug dealer, homie." Her minions laughed at her remark.

"She broke shit," said the attendant. "Doesn't want to pay." The gang leader said to him,

"Bet we can work out a way this *puta* (harlot) could pay you, *hombre*." She was ogling Nessa. "She looks pretty goddamn cute..."

John looked confused. Scratching his head, he was asking the attendant "How much does she owe?" when the gang leader threw her punch. The blow had been aimed at John, but Nessa got in the way.

She suffered the brunt of it. Doubling up in pain, she hit the ground as the gang leader, arm still extended, said to John, "*Cállate* (Shut up) fucker."

The gang leader seemed a tad remorseful for a brief moment as she was eying Nessa. She nodded at her crew, and they at once crossed toward the Oldsmobile.

Oh, shit, thought Nessa, and she grimaced when the gang took out their assorted weapons as they were swarming around John's car. One of the tough guys smashed one of the Oldsmobile's back windows. The rest of the gang joined in after a tough girl broke the front window on the passenger side.

Bats, chains, pipes, tire irons: they pounded the car with everything they carried. In the meantime, the gang leader seemed to be itching for a fight as she stood in front of John.

ONE HUNDRED PLACES

"Wait." Nessa had read her mind. "Just wait." She briefly looked at John, who frowned as he watched her struggling to get back on her feet. She limped toward the Oldsmobile.

"Nessa, no," he called out when she reached through the broken back-window of the car and pulled out his backpack. "No."

Nessa was already unzipping the backpack when the tough girl who had broken the front passenger-side window rushed around the front of the car and, seeing the backpack, yelled at the gang leader, "*Oye, patrona* (Hey, boss), look at this."

It was only money, thought Nessa as she pulled two wads of twenty-dollar bills out of the backpack. She handed them to the tough girl, who then extended her arm in the direction of the gas station attendant. He came to take the money.

"For your troubles, homie," the gang leader said from where she was standing. She came toward Nessa.

"No. Wait," Nessa said as the gang leader snatched the backpack from her and started dividing the rest of John's money among her crew.

Fuck, Nessa was thinking as she was stooping down to pick up the empty backpack, which had landed at her feet on the ground. She was lipping incoherencies to herself as she was straightening back up. Blind with fury, she made the mistake of spitting at the gang leader. The young woman's left hand smacked her across the face half a second later. One slap: that's all it was. But, God!, how it burned. Bitch, she had time to think as she fell to one knee.

One of the tough guys moved to strike her again.

"*Parale, bolitas* (Stop it, bolitas—nickname for someone who's obese)," the gang leader said to the tough guy. "She's paid for the damage." As the tough guy backed down, the gang leader, still holding on to the smug demeanor she'd maintained since her arrival, added, "No need for violence, *vato* (man, dude). Besides, why would you want to mess up such a pretty face?" She was laughing as she and her mob of boys-and-girls were regrouping and starting to head back the way they'd come. They had almost reached the edge of the road when the gang leader did a one eighty. She started back. Stopping half-way between her gang and Nessa, she spoke in Spanish when she said, "Get your act together, woman."

Nessa snorted. Get your act together, she thought. Easier said than done. She was still glaring at the young woman when she heard someone approach from behind her. It was John. He'd come to retrieve his backpack. He turned around to find the gas station attendant standing right in front of him, sizing him up.

Nessa thought John looked rather relieved when the attendant, after some heavy breathing through the nose, headed back the store. She was wincing and breathing heavy herself as she struggled to her feet. She stumbled into the Oldsmobile a few moments later, and when her door wouldn't close, John got out of the car and walked behind it to the other side. He spent some time trying to close the door—it was bent out of shape. He managed to close it. He started back the way he'd come, but then stopped. "That was my money," he said coming back to Nessa's door.

She looked up at him from the comfort of her seat. "And thank God for it," she said. "Solves all of our problems. Doesn't it?" John scratched the side of his neck. He breathed heavily, his shoulders rising and falling, as he headed back around the rear of the car. She heard the rush of air he let out through his mouth just before he got back behind the wheel. She was leaning forward on her seat. John got back on the nondescript road. Nessa looked in the rear-view mirror. The gas station was disappearing in the distance.

She flew forward—she wasn't wearing her seatbelt—when John slammed on the brakes. With only milliseconds to brace herself, her hands sprang out in front of her. They barely made the dashboard before her forehead smashed against the windshield. Luckily for her, the Oldsmobile was jerking forward at that very instant, and she was thrown back into her seat before she could suffer a real concussion. The gas station flashed by past her missing window. John had been making a U-turn. He was now speeding in the other direction, away from the city they didn't visit.

John was yelling his displeasure at Nessa as he drove in the late afternoon. "Why, in the hell, are you even here? You—all you do is do drugs and waste my money."

His swear words sounded clumsy, as if he didn't know how to chew someone out, Nessa thought. She was still feeling the residual effects of her earlier high. "Should I have let her beat you up?" she said, and John didn't answer. "Whatever, dude. I'm here for you." When John wrinkled his forehead, she told him, "You know you could not do this shit without me." She realized that he still looked confused; so, she tried to make it even clearer for him. "You can't even navigate your own life."

"I—" he said. "I was doing this, this shit—was doing just fine before I met you." The argument went on for several more minutes. At one point, when he glanced in her direction, she scowled at him and said straight to his face,

"You don't want me here? Let me leave. Pull the fuck over." John's face was one of surprise. "Yes," she said. "Just pull the fuck over." She had not expected him to follow through on this demand, but that was exactly what John did. He slammed on the brakes a second time and stopped right in the middle of the road.

"Well then, get—get the—heck—get the heck—out of here." He leaned sideways, but his seatbelt kept him from reaching to open her door. He straightened back on his seat and undid the buckle. As he went to lean over her lap, she reached for the handle and opened the door herself. Yes, she was taken aback, but she didn't give him another look. She turned to grab her things, but changed her mind. Slamming the front door shut as she exited, she retrieved her belongings through the rear door before marching to the side

101

of the road. The damaged door did not close. It clanked against the frame of the as John sped away.

The Oldsmobile squealing tires made Nessa turn to look. The car stopped suddenly in the middle of the road. John got out, and he looked angrier than she had ever seen him as he was coming around the front—as opposed to the back, as Lily had taught him—to the side of the road where she was standing. "Watch out!" she said, her heart racing. Another car screeched to a halt. It kissed the rear bumper of the Oldsmobile. John apparently didn't register any of this.

"You—you can't even close a car door," he yelled after he'd slammed the door shut. She cringed when, once again, the tires of the Oldsmobile squealed as he drove away. The car was disappearing in the distance when she started slogging along after it.

It was still several minutes before sunset, and an anxious-looking John was fidgeting as he sat behind the wheel. He was driving faster than he used to, his demeanor that of someone with a guilty conscience, which, given his inability to 'connect' with others, would be a first for him. He stared at the passenger seat awhile and had just gone back to minding the road when he squinted—as someone would who was trying to unravel a mystery. He looked at the seat again. There was a piece of paper tucked between the seat bottom and the backrest. He pulled over on the side of the road and reached for the paper. It was an envelope; the word 'Mom' was scribbled on it. He examined the envelope, and it was still open. He seemed reluctant to read the hand-written note he pulled out. As if operating on automatic, only seconds after he'd begun to read it, his hand reached into the glove compartment for a pen. He corrected two spelling mistakes in the first paragraph. But then a light seemed to go off in his head, and he stopped spell-checking. He continued reading after mumbling something to himself: something to the fact that Nessa—if it was true that she was going to be a journo—should have been a better speller. As he read, he clicked the pen in his free hand.

"Dear Mom:" Nessa had written. "It's been such a long time... I think you'd be glad to know I've left Antonio. Couldn't take it anymore. Right now, I'm traveling cross-country and trying to clean myself up (so far, I haven't succeeded).

"Met a man on the road the other day. Name's John. I promise. When this whole thing's done, I'll come visit—maybe I bring him along?

John stopped reading and scratched his head.

"Guess he's the closest thing to a real friend I've ever had. He's always bugging me about my habit… He's like you in this sense! "Those who care about you will make you cry. Isn't that what they say? :-)

"He's a bit weird though… (I'll tell you all about that in person).

John's eyes opened wide.

"But I think that if I stay around him long enough, I may actually beat this thing.

"You know what Mom? I think I may be falling for him. I know, I know. But I've known him for a several months now. What's long enough anyway?

"And do we really get to know anyone?

"I hope to see you soon! Love, V."

John's brow furrowed when he noticed the 'V' which followed the complimentary close. "Gosh darned," he said, a timid smile blossoming on his lips as he went to look in the rear-view mirror.

Nessa stared ahead at a darkening sky as she wandered along near the edge of the road. "Crybaby," she said to herself, her hands wiping tears off her cheeks with more roughness than was necessary. She turned to look behind her whenever she heard a vehicle approach. Sometimes, she would stick her hand out, her thumb up. She cursed when no one stopped.

At one point, as she was turning her head back in the direction she was going, she thought she saw a car approaching. It was coming the opposite way. Even though she couldn't make out the car too well in the twilight, she became excited when it seemed to her that it was slowing down.

John took his foot off the gas pedal and bent sideways to put the envelope with the note back where he'd found it. He saw Nessa when he straightened back behind the wheel.

Running to meet the car, Nessa stopped when she realized it was John who was approaching. Good boy, she thought. She was trying to fix herself up by running her fingers under her eyes. Her heart skipped a beat when the Oldsmobile drove past. "What the fu—?" she was in the middle of saying when the car made a U-turn.

"Didn't expect to see *you* here," she said leaning into the Oldsmobile through the front passenger-side door. "Don't you have places to see, landmarks to *drive by*?"

"*We* do," said John grinning. "Sorry I used the f-word." She was about to say something but didn't get the chance. "You're too much for me to handle, Nessa." Hiding a smile, she tried to make herself look angrier than she was.

"You're not an easy potato to peel either, John S. Peter." She did not sound as mean as she wanted to. John, for his part, came across as rather pleasantly surprised when he said, "You remember my name."

"Hasn't anyone ever explained to you how fussy you can be?" said she. She waited for him to interject. "Anyway. Why are you back?"

He averted his eyes before saying, "Because I like your company?" When he looked at her again, she was wondering whether she should believe him. He must have noticed the suspicion in her eyes, because he said, "And because I need someone to read my directions to me?"

"That's more like it!" she said chuckling as she took a few steps back and reached for the door handle. She was laughing inside when John leaned halfway out his window and signaled with his hand as he was getting back on the road: not only were the car's taillights broken, but there were no other vehicles around. "Don't you ever say 'fuck' in your mother's car again," she told him, and he said,

"Yes, Ma'am."

She said, "Don't you mean: 'No, ma'am?'"

"No, ma'am—I mean. Yes, ma'am, I mean 'No, ma'am.'"

They were silent for several moments, and then she said, "Where to next?"

"Seattle, I think," said John. He reached for his book, but she took hold of it first. After paging past the last Post-it-noted page, she said,

"You're right."

He seemed confused. "What do you m—?"

"That Washington *is* next."

"I just said that."

Nessa said, "That's not where we're going."

"No?" he said. "But that's where I'm driving to."

"In that case," she said, "you better stop right here." She was reaching for the door handle.

He was already fidgeting. "What?"

"I'm serious, John." She almost smiled.

"But..." John's voice trailed and looked sad as he slowed down on the side of the road.

Entering Texas—Nessa had changed John´s mind—they shared driving duties as they made their way to San Antonio via US-285S and I-10E. The two of them already ambling through the grounds of the Alamo by mid-morning the following day; John taking pictures as he went. Later in the day, after window shopping at River Center Mall, they strolled along both sides of the famous San Antonio River Walk.

The Oldsmobile was parked at Bathhouse Row, in Arkansas. It was several days later. John seemed at ease as he waited by himself in the car. Nessa looked refreshed, her hair wet, when she joined him moments later.

They arrived in Louisiana five days later, and spent a whole afternoon strolling through New Orleans' French Quarter. The sun was beginning to set as they ventured into a restaurant, where they enjoyed some of the city's Cajun food.

John drove through Great Smoky Mountains National Park, in Tennessee. During the drive, he stopped only twice on the side of the road. The first time, he stopped because he wanted to photograph some people who were fishing; the second, because Nessa made him, having decided, hours earlier, that she'd take a little walk the next time she needed a smoke. John could certainly use some alone time too, she figured. She took the wheel and drove through Shenandoah Valley, in Virginia, with the Blue Ridge mountains to her right and the Alleghenies to her left.

They arrived in Washington, D.C., and Nessa went to visit the Smithsonian Art Museum. While she was doing that, John was losing himself in the many exhibits at the National Air & Space Museum. He also took pictures of the Lincoln Memorial later that day as she sat down to watch the sunset from the top steps of the Memorial. Nightfall found them staring at the White House from their perch behind the floor-to-ceiling windows of a downtown D.C. café.

Under a cloudy sky a few days later, Nessa and John walked along the Boardwalk in Atlantic City, New Jersey. In Rhode Island, they followed the shoreline along Newport's 3.5-mile-long Cliff Walk National Recreation Trail. They made it to Massachusetts the following day, and visited Paul Revere

House and the Bunker Hill Monument at Boston National Historical Park.

Nessa crossed toward the bathroom of their motel room late that night, a towel draped around her torso. John lay in bed looking at the ceiling. A few of the beads of sweat that had gathered on his forehead began streaming down his temple and into his hair. He stayed like this awhile and fell asleep.

Nessa followed US-1 North and I-95 North. They arrived in New Hampshire. When she and John were riding up to the observatory atop Mt. Washington, it wasn't clear whether John was enjoying the stunning views as much as she was. He seemed much more relaxed on the way down. They continued north on Interstate 95; when they made it to Maine, they went straight to the Portland Head Lighthouse, where Nessa found a nice rock to sit on. She stayed there a long while looking at the sea while John spent his time quietly taking pictures. She had no idea that it was the first anniversary of Lily's death.

John's briefcase stood against the wall, under a medium-sized painting of purple lilacs adorning the motel room. "Don't tell me this is going to be your first time on an airplane," Nessa said to John, who was lying in bed next to her. He nodded, and she said, "Aren't you afraid—even a little?"

"Not me," he said at the same time that he was negating with his head. "But Ma was." Which Nessa did not find at all surprising; for she, too, was afraid of flying. "Sometimes she had bad dreams about it."

She corrected him, saying, "Nightmares."

"Same thing," said he. "Her dreams were usually of her dying in a plane crash."

She snickered, and John said, "I think she knew there was no logical explanation for those *nightmares*." He made a funny face at her as he was emphasizing the last word. "But she always said I didn't have to worry about it myself."

"Okay…," said Nessa not understanding. "How so?"

"I find that she was right," said John. "I've seen hundreds—no, probably it's been thousands—of planes fly above my town. Not one of them has ever fallen from the sky."

"Within your field of view that is," she said, "or that you know of."

"Still," said John. "Why worry about stuff like that?" She thought, Uh? And he must have read the confusion in her face. "When your time comes," he said, "it won't matter where you are." Right… she thought. "It's not as if we could hide."

Resting the side of her face on the palm of her hand, she said, "It isn't even funny how you're not afraid of dying." John was grinning. "And yet, when it comes to dealing with people…" He sounded defensive when he interjected.

"I'm not afraid of people either."

"You aren't?!"

"It's just that they're not normal." He paused briefly. "I mean—"

His choice of words surprised her. She said, "They're not normal? Don't you mean—?"

"I mean, they're not like me."

"We—everyone—is different."

"Sometimes it's too difficult just being around them," he said. She didn't know what to say to that. "That's what Ma said." Ah, thought Nessa. She understood now. "Ma said that it was better if I put it in those terms; that it would make more sense to me that way."

What a great person Lily must have been! Nessa cast down her eyes as this idea started her thinking of her own mother.

"Did you know," he said, "that there are more than a few million people like me out there?"

"I know," she lied. "I've known about Aspies for some time now." Moving closer to him, she tried a little kiss. John obliged. "Everybody's…"

"Different?" he said. "I'm normal after all. Aren't I?" He grinned, and she found it cute that he could laugh at his own expense.

"Yep," she said. "You are.—Just like those few million other Aspies out there!"

They made their way back to Massachusetts, had a quick lunch, and went to visit the John F. Kennedy Presidential Museum and Library. They then spent the afternoon ambling about at the Boston Public Garden.

Following an early dinner, Nessa led John to Bay Village, where she not only dragged him into Jacques' Cabaret, but also talked him in to accompanying her in trying several of the beers on offer there. John wasn't being his old, talkative self by the time nine o'clock rolled around, and she ended up doing most of the talking—and drinking—the rest of the time while enjoying the live entertainment. She was in the dark about it being John's birthday that day; just as she had been about it having been the one-year anniversary of Lily's death the day before.

Nessa did not have her fill at Jacques'. It was her reason for stopping to get a six-pack on the way back to the hotel. She ended up drunk. John helped her to the bathroom after all the alcohol she'd ingested collided with the seafood she'd consumed earlier, and her stomach said 'Enough.' He set her hands around the toilet bowl and left her there while he went back into the bedroom. He came back with two pillows, one of which he placed under her behind; the other, on the edge of the bathtub. He sat down. A half-hour had passed by the time John placed a hand on her shoulder.

Nessa's upper body was nestled in John's arms as they slept in the bathtub, where they'd ended up spending the night.

John awoke when an alarm went off somewhere outside the bathroom. "Oh, shoot," he said. "Nessa. Wake up." He was shaking her. She half-opened her eyes, and he said, "We have to go." He removed himself from under her and left the bathroom. A few moments later, the sound of the alarm stopped.

Still feeling druggy, Nessa tried to pull herself out of the bathtub. She fell back. John helped her out of it when he returned. Could you be more disheveled? she thought as she looked at herself in the mirror. They went into the bedroom and started gathering their belongings.

The sun was beginning to rise.

As the Oldsmobile crawled along in stop-and-go traffic, through the windshield Nessa could see the airport ahead in the distance. The briefcase with John's money was in the rear seat. She glanced at it.

John had parked in the airport garage. He exited the car and stood in front of it waiting for Nessa. They were heading toward the terminal building a few moments later when he said, "Do you want to hold it—?"

"May I?" Nessa was saying even before he'd finished his sentence, and she did a little dance when John nodded. As they continued toward the lobby, the briefcase kept swinging back and forth in her hand, and they were almost at the security checkpoint when it fell open. The money spilled onto the floor.

She dropped the briefcase—it was close to empty now—at her side and got on her knees. Opening her arms wide, she tried to gather all the money at once, but the bills were scattered all over the place.

A police officer was ordering coffee from a stand nearby as passengers gawked at the scene. John had stooped down to help.

ONE HUNDRED PLACES

Nessa didn't like the way the customs agent was looking at her from behind his rather clean desk. Come on, she thought. That's way more suspicion than the situation calls for. She looked at John some moments. It seemed as if their unscheduled detour hadn't fazed him even half as much as it had her.

John had been looking at the ceiling—from where a dozen model airplanes hung—from the time the police officer had delivered them to the Customs Service.

"We have no reason to believe the money isn't yours," the agent was saying, and since she was the only one paying any attention to him, Nessa said,

"It's not mine." She pointed at John. "It's his."

"The money is mine, officer," John said. His eyes remained fixed on the planes.

"We have no reason to believe it isn't," the agent said to Nessa, "but as our security cameras show, you were the one carrying it." She let a rush of air out through her mouth. "Unless you show us some proof you paid taxes on that money," continued the agent, "I can't legally allow you to take it out of the state." The hell, she thought. "I'm afraid you're going to have to miss that plane, Miss…"

"Vanessa. Name's Vanessa." She'd managed to sound much less pissed than she was.

"Miss Vanessa," said the agent.

She looked at John. He was grinning for some reason.

John sat by a window. He was in the ticketing area of the airport, looking at the traffic jam that was forming on the road just outside the lobby. Behind him, at the other end of the lobby, was Nessa. She was on edge as she stepped away from the ticket counter.

"I thought your name was Nessa," John said to her as she neared him. There was a half-grin on his face. Perhaps he remembered the 'V' in the note she'd written to her mother?

111

"It's what I prefer to be called," she said. "But my proper name is Vanessa." She exhaled through her mouth a couple of times. "Sorry I made us lose the flight." Right at that very moment, she felt genuine concern for John, for his wellbeing. "You're sure you're going to be okay all by yourself?" she said. "I'm afraid y—"

"Why are you afraid?" John said. "I was going to visit him by myself anyway had I not met you."

"But you are going to *come back*, right?" She had to admit it to herself: she was feeling a hint of jealousy. "Don't go falling for one of those strippers out there." John was grinning. "No detours. Okay?"

He nodded at the question, then shook his head from side to side. "You have my money," he said. "I have to come back."

She said, "I hope you're kidding."

"No," he said, and she made a face. "Yes?"

"Phew." She smiled. "For a minute there, I thought I'd lost my special friend." Had John been any better at reading emotions, she thought, he would've seen something in the way she was looking at him (It was one of those looks…); he would've, at the very least, seen the wonder in her eyes as she stared into his. But it was no use—and this, she knew—for, as brilliant as John was in so many other areas, he just couldn't read a person's face. And what was yet more troubling to her: on the whole subject of emotional intelligence, it seemed, he was illiterate.

"When I come back," John said, "we'll go to New York to see the last two places."

"I'd very much like that." Standing so close to him, she did not have to reach too far to run her hand along the side of his torso and down to the hip area.

Back at the security area, Nessa held the briefcase in front of her, both hands on the handle. She was standing by waiting for John to pass through a metal detector. John stared at the metal detector several moments. Starting to move closer, he turned around before reaching it. Nessa didn't see him waving at her. She was digging in her bag at that very moment. He kept going.

"John," she called. "Wait." She pulled out of her bag a small package wrapped in funny-looking paper. It was the same package she had been putting in her bag when she went to sit down for coffee at Powell's City of Books—back in Portland. She started toward one of two officers who were working security, and as she went to hand over the package, the officer, instead of taking the package, frowned at her. "Could you give this to him please?" Nessa said while pointing toward John.

"Sorry, ma'am," the female security officer said. "Not allowed."

Nessa cringed when she heard the officer's voice. Poor woman, she thought. Getting closer to the woman, she said something to her in a whisper. She even made a 'pretty-please?' face at her. And the officer did roll her eyes, but she obliged.

"Here, John," the latter was saying seconds later in that falsetto Nessa had found so utterly annoying. A look of confusion washed over John's face as he accepted the package from the 'unknown' woman, who said at the same time as Nessa,

"Happy Birthday, John!"

John's eyes darted from Nessa—she was rolling her eyes at the woman's voice—to the officer and back again as he flashed a big smile. He seemed genuinely surprised. "But it was yesterday," he said to the security officer, who, having already turned on her heels and started minding the other passengers, didn't seem to have heard him.

"I know," Nessa said. "I'm sorry."

John said to her, "Wait for me at the hotel, okay?" and she nodded. "We'll finish the book when I come back. Then we do it again, backwards!"

"Yes, John," she said once she was able to stop the hearty laugh that had issued from her. She had not laughed like this in a long while, and she felt herself blush as hope at the prospect of happiness radiated from her being.

"Now, John," the security officer said, "you should get the heck out of here before I confiscate that package."

John's eyes opened wide. He held the package closer to him as if he were afraid the woman would actually confiscate it. When he turned toward Nessa, she and his briefcase were already gone. He pivoted on the heel of one foot and faced the metal detector once again. He gulped.

The sun was shining against the left side of the Boeing 767 as it accelerated down the runway. The airplane rotated thirty seconds later; a minute after that, it was banking and heading due west.

The plane leveled off about ten minutes into the flight. John was unwrapping his gift. He smiled when he saw the book. '*The World Edition of One Hundred Places to See Before You Die.*'

A woman in business attire stirred in her sleep on the seat next to John's. She opened her eyes momentarily and saw him staring.

"Are you on a road trip too?" he said to her.

The woman said, "California? Seen it a million times. All I want to do now is sleep." Not catching her verbal cue, John kept talking.

"Are you tired?" he said.

"Been gone for a month on business," said the businesswoman. "I'm so damn tired right now, I don't even remember what day it is."

John said, "You're not a tourist?"

"On business," she said. "Get it?" She looked straight at him for a whole second before turning away from him and closing her eyes.

"It's Tuesday," John said.

114

ONE HUNDRED PLACES

"I know it's Tuesday," said she. "Are you mad or something? What's wrong with you!"

John—incapable of helping himself—said in one breath, "Day eleven, month nine, second year of the new millennium. The time is zero eight fifteen."

"I've got it. I've got it." She was glaring at him now. "Could you please shut up?"

A chime was heard throughout the cabin, and the woman pointed and said, "Look. The seatbelt sign just went off." John looked about him; it seemed he didn't understand what she meant. "Why don't you go for a walk or something?"

"I almost finished my book," he said.

"Oh," said she. "You a writer."

John fished in his backpack. He brought out his old book and showed it to her. "Only two more places to go to." Replacing the book in the backpack, he said, "I'll see them when I come back."

It was several minutes later, and skyscrapers and city streets could be seen through the broken clouds as the businesswoman slept placidly in her seat. It seemed that the plane was on its final approach.

From his vantage point mid-cabin, John could see out through one of the windows on the left side of the airplane. He shook his head from side to side, as if in disbelief, and did a double take when the World Trade Center Towers appeared intermittently through breaks in the clouds. He looked rather confused; nevertheless, he fetched his by-now-tattered book out of his backpack.

Having already check-marked page number ninety-nine, he was about to close the book when the plane banked to the right and the Statue of Liberty appeared beyond a window on the right side of the plane. She was too far away to satisfy any but the least discerning of souls, but John made something like an 'Oh-well' face. He smiled to himself at the same time that the fingers of his right hand were rushing through to the last page on his book, and he was beaming with joy when he marked it off. He let out a deep sigh as he closed the book. From that moment on, he seemed both lost in thought and at peace with himself.

One hundred places. Yes, Lily would be proud.

At the same time that John had been check-marking the last two pages in his book, rain clouds had been drifting over the Boston cityscape.

A taxicab dropped Nessa off in front of a nice hotel. As she scurried in through revolving doors and went inside, the cab drove away too fast. Autumn leaves whirled in eddies of wind.

Inside the airplane, John was thumbing through every page in his old book. It was as if he needed to make sure every one of those pages had been marked. He pressed the book against his chest and smiled a Mona Lisa smile.

He didn't notice the commotion in the forward cabin.

The windows of the hotel room where Nessa was staying looked dusty from the inside. John's briefcase lay open on top of the bed, the money scattered all of over the place as if someone had thrown it up in the air like confetti. The TV was on. It showed a newscast in progress that was being interrupted by staff who hurried to and fro in the vicinity of the anchor. A production assistant handed a couple of pages to the anchor, who turned pale as he scanned the document. The anchor gave an almost-imperceptible gulp to the air about him before he got the nerve to look back at the camera.

"We interrupt this newscast…" he said as he began serving the breaking-news report.

Syringes still in their packaging lay on the night table as Nessa, oblivious to the sights and sounds around her, sat in bed tapping the inside of her right arm. A light drizzle began to fall over the city.

"Right now, there are unconfirmed reports that at least two airplanes have crashed into the World Trade Center towers," the news anchor said. "We are getting ready to bring you up to date. Please, stay tuned." He gulped as he was shifting his weight on the chair and looking off camera.

The sound of paper peeling away.

Nessa was unwrapping a syringe.

The news anchor shuffled his papers and spent some time fiddling with his ear-piece or otherwise adjusting it. Fidgety, he seemed to be killing time and trying to gather his thoughts. How could anyone make sense of what they were about to broadcast?

Nessa was about to stick the needle in her arm when her eyes began taking in everything in her field of view.

"And now, some breaking news," the anchor said. "As we speak, something terrible is happening in downtown Manhattan." A sigh escaped him. "It seems that multiple airliners have crashed into the World Trade Center."

The needle pierced Nessa's skin just as her eyes came to rest on the TV. She heard the anchor's voice just as she was catching a glimpse of the images in front of her. The twin Towers, she thought, and she closed and opened her eyes repeatedly.

"Flights eleven, seventy-seven, and one seventy-five," the news anchor said. "All three have reportedly crashed into the World Trade Center towers."

The syringe, its needle trapped under her skin, hung from Nessa's arm as she stared at the inferno depicted on the TV. An overpowering lethargy overcame her. She froze. Moments later, she rose and dragged herself closer to the TV. Was she seeing things? Had she heard right?

Several moments of confusion followed, and then the enormity of what was happening hit her. "Fuck, fuck, fuck!" she yelled at the top of her lungs. "Oh, God. Oh, God. Oh,

God." She bent forward and set her hands just above the knees.

"Oh, my God!" It was almost a whisper. Her eyes had fixed on the flight numbers of the three doomed airliners. They were scrolling past at the bottom of the screen.

She began to sob, and for the first time she felt the sting of the syringe in her arm. Yanking it out, she hurled it across the room at the window. Her blood ran in rivulets down her forearm and splashed onto the up-to-that-point-pristine, sand-beige carpet.

Twilight. Rain hit the windows as Nessa convulsed face down in bed. Unable to come to terms with reality, she cried her heart out. It was all she could do. Hours and hours of crying as, outside, rain washed the windows. Night came and went, and a new day arrived. She couldn't move. Only late on the second night did she give any sign of life when she turned herself onto her back. Inconsolable, she stared at the ceiling.

It was two days later. She still had not left the hotel room; neither had she eaten anything. Ravaged with grief, she made herself sit up. She rocked back and forth at the edge of the bed, her hands clasped between her knees. She cried for several more moments.

The clouds began to break outside. She sniffed as she wiped the tears away with the back of her hand. Slowly, she began to pull herself together. She trembled as she was reaching for the phone.

Hesitant fingers punched in some numbers. There was a ring at the other end a few moments later. The line rang several more times as she was getting to her feet and moving toward the window. Her steps felt heavy.

"*Bueno?*" said a female voice at the other end. It said, "Hello?" two seconds later. Nessa looked out the window, at patches of blue sky, and said tentatively,

"Mom."

ONE HUNDRED PLACES

THE END
<<<<>>>>

PEDRO VASQUEZ

DEAR READER:

Thank you so much for reading my second novel. I would also appreciate it if you took a few minutes to review it—if you're so inclined.

ACKNOWLEDGMENTS

Many thanks to S.J. Johnson, my shipmate, for coming up with an excellent idea for a screenplay; and to my partner in crime, S.P. Shepherd, for her support and advice.

ONE HUNDRED PLACES

ABOUT THE AUTHOR

Pedro Vasquez, a self-published novelist, is also a former US Navy Sailor and screenwriter. He began writing movie scripts after retiring from the military in 2012. His favorite past times are going to the movies, listening to music, and reading--not necessarily in that order. When he's not traveling the world, he likes spending time with his family, whom he adores. And he does travel often; he enjoys flying so much, that he once got on twenty-seven flight-segments, in just thirty days! Pedro spent the first several years of his naval career working as a jet engine mechanic, after which he "crossed ratings" and became a translator. A polyglot, besides English and Spanish (his native language) he also speaks basic Albanian and Indonesian. Next on his list of languages to learn is Mandarin.